David Burnell was born and br
ics at Cambridge University, t
and then spent his career ap
problems in the Health Service, coal mining and battery ....
industry. On "retiring" he completed a PhD at Lancaster University on the deeper meaning of data from London's water meters.

He and his wife live in Berkshire but own a small holiday cottage in North Cornwall. They have four grown-up children.

Perils and Predicaments

Full-length "Cornish Conundrums" by David Burnell

Doom Watch: *"Cornwall and its richly storied coast has a new writer to celebrate in David Burnell. His crafty plotting and engaging characters are sure to please crime fiction fans." Peter Lovesey*

Slate Expectations: *"combines an interesting view of an often overlooked side of Cornish history with an engaging pair of sleuths who follow the trail from past misdeeds to present murder." Carola Dunn*

"An original atmospheric setting, which is sure to put Delabole on the map. A many-stranded story keeps the reader guessing, with intriguing local history colouring events up to the present day." Rebecca Tope

Looe's Connections: *"History, legend, and myth mixed with a modern technical conundrum make this an intriguing mystery." Carola Dunn*

"A super holiday read set in a super holiday location!" Judith Cutler

Tunnel Vision: *"Enjoyable reading for all who love Cornwall and its dramatic history." Ann Granger*

Peter Lovesey *has won the Crime Writer's Association Cartier Diamond Dagger. His most dogged detective is Superintendent Peter Diamond.*

Carola Dunn *is author of the Daisy Dalrymple and Cornish mysteries.*

Rebecca Tope *writes the Cotswold and West Country Mysteries.*

Judith Cutler *is author of several crime series, most recently featuring Detective Superintendant Fran Harman.*

Ann Granger *authors several crime series, most recently the Campbell and Carter mysteries.*

ONE SCOOP OR TWO?

David Burnell

SKEIN BOOKS

ONE SCOOP OR TWO?

Published by Skein Books, 88, Woodcote Rd, Caversham, Reading

First edition: September 2016.

This book, although set in real locations, is entirely a work of fiction. Background events, such as the disaster at Levant Tin Mine in 1919, and arguments about computers at Harwell, really happened. But no fictional character is based on any real person, living or dead. Any resemblance is purely coincidental.

ISBN-13: 978-1537183220
ISBN-10: 1537183222

The front cover shows the cottage of Anne Hathaway (William Shakespeare's wife) just outside Stratford on Avon. Cover photographs were taken by my wife, Marion.

FOREWORD

It's tempting, isn't it? All those tubs of ice cream, some the old favourites you had as a child and some with flavours you've never heard of. They sound delicious so why not try a couple?

I hope this book of short stories might evoke similar feelings. Maybe you've read one or two of my *Cornish Conundrums* and want to try something shorter. Many of these tales involve some sort of crime but only one or two reach as far as murder.

You'll meet a variety of story tellers. William Shakespeare pens us a couple of reminiscences of his early years. Tales of a young George Gilbert, long before *Conundrums*, from her student days at Cambridge; and of Robbie Glendenning at sixth form, already shaping up to be an investigative journalist. Plus a constable from Scarborough, Lauren Shaw, who made a previous appearance in my first book of short stories, *Pebbles on the Shore*.

No African tales this time. But they range from the beginning of human time to the near future. Of the rest, two are from the 1500s, several from the twentieth century and the rest are "present day".

Discerning readers may spot that the author's summer holidays were spent on the Orkneys and North Scotland. The stories cover the oldest village in Europe, the largest sea cave in the UK, approval for the first commercial computer, help with an old mathematical assertion and the recent European Referendum.

Perils and Predicaments

Others deal with golf, croquet and the antics of a contortionist.

Can you spot which is which from their titles?

In short, plenty of perils and predicaments to choose from and relish. You will find some sort of "scoop" in every one.

As always, I am grateful to my circle of critical friends for their suggested improvements and corrections. Any errors that remain are my own. But I'd like to improve further. Contact me via my website.

David Burnell   website: davidburnell.info
September 2016

CONTENTS

Page

The present-day garden of Hampton Court Palace

1.   AGENT OF THE CROWN

Her Majesty held out a hand in regal welcome. 'Come, young man, we do not have long. But there is no need for fear.'

I knew not what she meant. It was early 1585. A courtier had appeared and summoned me to Hampton Court. 'Secrecy is of the essence.' Two weeks later I found myself in the Royal Palace.

'I need someone educated,' the Queen pronounced, 'unknown to the world but able to improvise and to communicate. A man who would glory in serving his Sovereign, at home or abroad.'

I gulped. 'Your Majesty, I would be proud to be that man. But my languages are modest. I was taught Latin, the language of priests; and I learned some Spanish. I declare: I have no knowledge of diplomacy.'

'Young man, my courtiers all think diplomacy is a form of cheating. You will acquire real diplomatic skills as you go. And you will report directly to me. Now, what do you know of Spain?'

A month later I was a Crown agent, jolting in stunned apprehension to Spain.

Sir Francis Walsingham, the Queen's Head of Intelligence, had terrified me with the grisly details of the Inquisition. I resolved I was not going any closer to King Philip of Spain than was necessary. Navarre, in Northeast Spain, on a major coach route, was close enough. I had handled stage coaches in Stratford; soon I found employment at the Hispaniola Tavern in Navarre.

At first, when not at work, I kept myself aloof, writing sonnets in my garret as I refined a Basque-accented Spanish. I garbed myself in local clothing and disciplined myself never to speak in my mother tongue. Before long I was seen as native to the area.

But I was not idle. Gradually I shared the company and the gossip of my fellow-workers. From the porter I learned that diplomatic mailbags passed through Navarre en route to Paris and the couriers stayed the night at the Hispaniola. Further research revealed a weekly pattern in each direction.

So what happened, I wondered, to the bags overnight? I befriended a bedroom maid so no-one would question my presence inside the Hispaniola and over time examined every room.

But the breakthrough came when one of the regular couriers, whom by now I knew well, asked me to take his pouch to the tavern-keeper while he repaired a broken rein.

I was excited to have a signal from the King of Spain in my hands. How I longed to break open the pouch and read his secrets but I managed to resist. Dutifully, I handed it over to the tavern-keeper and noted that it was put away in a safe in the far wall. What I needed now was access - regular access - to the key.

Then a message reached me from Walsingham. 'Makest thou progress? Else return at once.' Time was not on my side.

To exert leverage on the tavern-keeper I had been looking for ways of exploiting his reputed affair with the cook. For months it had been the talk of the tavern. But this would take too long.

6

Then, on a minor dalliance of my own in the stable, as I scooped her up into my arms, the bedroom maid asked, 'Why mightest our master have a key hidden beneath his bed?'

It was not certain this was a spare key to the safe, but it seemed likely. As far as I knew there was not much else of value in the Hispaniola. But if it was kept hidden and never used, then could it be replaced by another key that looked much the same, so the theft remained undetected?

I stood in a position where I was likely to be proffered the diplomatic bag again. The third time I was given it and took it in I spotted the key on the desk, waiting to be used. It was brass but not over-elaborate. Where might I find one which looked much like it?

I recalled coming across a locksmith on one of my errands to Navarre. Visiting him again, I spotted keys of a similar type on display. Taking courage, I went in.

'Sire, the mistress of the Hispaniola hast ordered me to purchase her a new lock.'

'Verily, we have locks: peruse our selection.'

I looked and made my choice. 'This one 'twill serve her purpose. But she insists her husband never be told.' I said no more but my eyes hinted at domestic disharmony.

A few days later the tavern-keeper and his wife had to attend a local feast. They would be late home; it was the chance I'd been waiting for. By the time the pair returned, in something of a stupor, the spare safe-key had been swapped with the one I had bought earlier.

At last I was in a position to read the diplomatic traffic.

For months all went smoothly. By day I welcomed the stage coaches, dealt with the travellers and cared for the horses. By night, twice a week, I sidled into the tavern-keeper's office and inspected the diplomatic mail. And once a week I despatched a summary report to Walsingham and hence the Queen. Oh the joy of once more deploying my mother tongue!

I learned much. I was one of the first to know that the Spanish Admiral, Santa Cruz, had died; and been replaced by the Duke of Medina. And the diplomatic replies told me that the Duke's expertise was as a soldier not a sailor: he had never been to sea in his life.

My report on this aberration waxed eloquent.

A year later I learned that the Spanish fleet was gathering in Cadiz. This information, coupled with the known naval weakness of Medina, allowed Sir Francis Drake to launch an audacious raid on the Spanish fleet at anchor, which set their designs back a year.

Later I observed the development of plans to combine the Spanish fleet with an army in Holland. I was able to pass on the inside story on the first, disastrous sailing of the Armada in April 1588, when a storm meant the fleet did not even reach the English Channel. Fortunately I could expand the terse descriptions in the raw signals into something full of high drama.

And I warned the Queen in advance of the second sailing in July. England could not complain it was caught unawares.

All this time I knew I was playing a dangerous game; my luck could not last. I had almost been caught in the tavern-keeper's office when the man returned from a late-night liaison with the cook. Now I sensed I was being watched in turn. Fear of the methods of the Inquisition, applied ruthlessly to my tender body, made it hard to sleep.

So it was a relief to receive the command from Walsingham: 'Thy task is completed. Return at once.'

I had made plans for such an instruction. Whenever I put the stage coaches away I always noted any with empty luggage racks, in which I might stow away. Providentially there was one that very night.

Early next morning I was out of Navarre and across the border to France before the tavern-keeper was even awake. But my sudden exit was tantamount to a confession: if caught I knew I would receive no mercy. Next night I discarded the first stage coach and moved on to a second.

I was out of Aquitaine while the search was still underway in Navarre. A week later I had reached Calais and hired a small fishing boat to take me home.

I did not expect a rousing welcome on my return. I knew from the start that my role as an agent of the Queen was low profile. But I did expect recognition from Walsingham; and to be told the impact of my many disclosures.

What I had not expected was that others would have acted on my findings without giving them (and me) any credit whatsoever.

Sir Francis Drake's raid on Cadiz had, apparently, been on his own initiative. Nothing much had been done, by the forewarned English, to tackle the Armada as it sailed up the Channel. The Armada had moored at Calais to take on board the Dutch soldiers. But Drake's navy blocked their way back and they had to return round the north of Scotland. It was another storm which finally smashed the Armada, not naval mastery or first-class intelligence.

'At least,' I mused, 'I could publish some raunchy memoirs.'

I had seen a lot in the last three years; and my writing skills had blossomed.

But Walsingham was adamant. 'William, an agent's role is always secret. Nothing must ever be said about your time away.'

Which was the reason that I turned from reports of life and death for my country to writing plays. It seemed not to have been done before. I could convey some of the affairs of state in a fictional form.

One of my first plays was a light romantic comedy set in Navarre. I had gone forth as an act of love to my Queen but my labour had been largely unrecognised.

'Love's Labour's Lost' was the right title as far as I was concerned.

Historians can find no official trace of William Shakespeare from the birth of his twins in 1585 to his appearance in London in 1592.

2. THE RIDDLE OF SKARA BRAE

The crowd of visitors hung on every word of the young Guide, whose lapel badge told them was called Richard.

'You are about to see Neolithic Skara Brae, the oldest known village in Europe,' he told them.

'And these guys here have got some damnably old places to compete with,' observed an American visitor on the front row to his wife Elmina in a loud whisper. 'That Kirkwall where we stayed last night is pretty old – Nordic, didn't they say? I can believe the hotel goes back that far. The plumbing certainly does.'

'Homer, dear, the hotel is Victorian.'

'But who came first – Mr Norr Dick or Mr Victor Ian?'

Outwardly the Guide was calm but in his mind his eyes rolled. He had to put up with this level of ignorance day after day. For someone just starting a PhD in Geology it was hard to take.

'The village is a World Heritage Site – one of only four in Scotland. It was uncovered in the 1850s,' he explained. 'There was a huge storm one winter which scooped the sand off the dunes. The village had been lying protected beneath. No-one took much notice for a long time. It needed carbon dating to determine its age. They reckon it's about five thousand years old.'

'How does that work?' asked a precocious looking youngster, also on the front row. He looked in danger of being suffocated by the huge Americans.

An intelligent question from a serious listener - Richard was overjoyed. He was about to launch into a full explanation and then lost heart. He couldn't make it simple enough to make sense within the American's world view.

'Stick close to me, son, I'll tell you as we go round.'

'So will we see the pots and pans they used in those times?' asked Elmina.

'I'm afraid we won't,' answered Richard, thankful that at least she hadn't asked about dishwashers. 'You see, that's the riddle of Skara Brae. When the village was found it was not just deserted, it was abandoned. For some reason or other the inhabitants had moved on, taking most of their belongings with them. But no-one knows why.'

'So you're charging us £8 a head to go see a place that you've not even figured out yet?' Homer sounded mutinous.

Elmina was conscious that her husband's diplomacy was wafer thin at the best of times and had been made worse by recent indigestion. She turned to the Guide. 'I'm sure you must have worked it out. What's the solution?'

Richard's spirit rose a little. He would have told them anyway but it was much better to be asked.

'When the village was first unearthed, it was thought some natural disaster had caused them all to flee. Exactly what was not clear. The wilder ideas ranged from a tsunami to a large meteor.'

The audience were listening hard. You could have heard a pin drop.

'Of course, the climate on the Orkneys has changed over time. It's hard to believe but many years ago it was hot. So another theory was that the population might have fled from a wild fire that threatened but in the end didn't hit them.'

12

The precocious youngster was following anyway. 'We learnt about Pompeii at school. That was destroyed by an erupting volcano. Could that have been the reason?'

'It's a clever idea. But there's no trace of larva around here, so probably not,' Richard responded.

'So what d'you think?' asked Elmina.

'Oh, it was some form of natural disaster,' said the Guide confidently. 'My money's on a disease that came on them suddenly – like the Black Death in Medieval Britain, but much earlier. The survivors might take their belongings and escape by boat.' He laughed, 'They might have been the first Americans.'

This seemed to stun the audience. No further questions from the couple in the front row. The idea that they might be descendants of refugees from this primitive village was unthinkable.

'Anyway, that's enough talking,' said Richard. 'Let's walk along and see the village.'

That evening Homer and Elmina swapped notes with Louise, an American lady at their hotel in Kirkwall. She had spent the day on a coach tour of the southern islands, visiting the Italian Chapel and later the Tomb of Eagles. The Neolithic village was for tomorrow.

'Skara Brae is a good day out,' said Elmina. 'You'll enjoy it. Mind, the village is smaller than I expected. It's more like a series of connecting burrows. They couldn't have been very tall five thousand years ago. But hang on to the Guide: he tells a good tale.'

Louise was equally complementary about the Italian Chapel. 'Built by Prisoners of War, see. I guess it made a change from standing in freezing water, building links between the islands. It's odd, you know. When the Japanese did that sort of thing we called it a War Crime.'

It was a point of view. No doubt there was a good answer but no-one knew what it was. She went on to describe the Tomb of Eagles, which raised other unanswerable questions.

The next evening the three met again. 'You're right about small,' said Louise. 'If the Guide had told us the village was the home of the Seven Dwarves I'd have believed him.'

'And all abandoned because of the growth to a bigger society,' she added.

'I don't think so,' responded Homer. 'We pushed our Guide. He reckoned it was some early plague that forced 'em to flee.'

'Our man, Richard, was quite clear,' said Louise, puzzled. 'He pointed to a change in the wider society. It had moved on from being isolated communities to some sort of clan system. In other words, he said, the inhabitants at Skara Brae left as they'd decided there was more safety in numbers.'

'Perhaps it was a different Richard, Homer.' Elmina knew her husband could paint himself into a corner with his dogmatic arguing. She'd lost several friends that way. Best not to push things too far.

'Or maybe he'd got more up to date research,' said Louise.

'It can't have changed that much since yesterday,' protested Homer. He sulked a little, brooding, as the conversation moved on to the Italian Chapel.

Next morning Homer announced that he was going back to

14

Skara Brae for a resolution. Elmina had already committed herself to exploring St Magnus's Cathedral at Kirkwall with Louise, so he was on his own.

Richard spotted him in the distance, waddling determinedly from the Skara Brae car-park wearing a tee shirt emblazoned "Homer Sapiens", and decided (understandably) to take precautions.

A few minutes later, as Homer once again placed himself on the front row, he was surprised to see a Guide with a small moustache, dark glasses and a baseball cap, name tag "Harold", about to address them.

Homer had come prepared with plenty of questions. He'd been planning them on the journey. But this was, apparently, a new Guide altogether. 'What's happened to Richard?'

'Richard isn't well today. I'll do my best to cover.' This Guide, "Harold", spoke with a transatlantic accent and looked rather tense.

Homer was temporarily silenced.

'You're about to see the oldest village in Europe,' "Harold" continued. 'They reckon it was first in use around 3200 BC and occupied until 2500 BC. That makes it older than the Pyramids in Egypt.'

'Only if you're correct on the dates,' asserted Homer. He had decided that today he was going to question everything.

'Carbon dating is accurate to the nearest century, Mr Sapiens. On my PhD I had to study it in detail.'

Homer did not know if the Guide realised that "Sapiens" was only a joke. There was silence from the floor.

The Guide continued, 'No, the riddle of Skara Brae is not the dates, it's why the place was abandoned – almost like the Mary Celeste.'

'Hey, your predecessor told us, two days ago, that it was the result of a plague. Then yesterday the same man blamed it on the development of a wider society.'

Others in the audience had also conversed with recent visitors. 'The day before that it was some sort of fire.' Other possibilities were also being muttered. Even dinosaurs were in the frame.

Homer felt strengthened. 'You guys need to make up your minds. Or else bring in someone from the States who knows what they're talking about.'

The Guide clenched his fists and swallowed hard. If he was provoked much more . . . He would lose his summer job if he throttled Homer, no doubt, but it might well be worth it.

They wouldn't be able to pin it on him, anyway. It would all be blamed on the mysterious "Harold".

Maybe he could ask Homer to step outside? The man was big but he was pretty sure that was all flab. Just tripping him up would be some source of satisfaction.

Or maybe he could entice him into a burrow at Skara Brae? There was a good chance he'd be stuck there for ever - long enough to teach him a lesson, anyway.

But Richard was saved from personal disaster by an intervention from the back row from an American lady, tidily dressed and confident.

'Hey, Homer, you don't know enough to challenge a Guide. And anyway, what happened to the American tradition of courtesy?'

With effort Homer managed to turn on the bench and face his

16

new opponent. 'Who the hell are you?' he asked testily.

'My name is Hosanna Hoskyns. I'm Visiting . . . Professor of Myth and Legend, Edinburgh University.'

There was a longer silence. A Professor from the United States was beyond him. Homer had met his match.

Richard took the chance to chat to his saviour on the way back from the site.

'It's hard work, Hosanna. Trouble is, all these guys want is a firm answer.'

'That might be 'cos you're pitching it wrong.'

'Ugh? How d'you mean?'

'Well you're a scientist. You like proofs and answers. So when you tell them it's a "riddle" and they ask for the solution, your instinct is to oblige. You pick a different one each day. Which is fine till they swap notes in the evenings. As they do – there's not much else on offer in the Orkneys.'

'OK. Charge accepted. But what's the alternative?'

'In other contexts people are very happy when the solution is unknown. The Loch Ness Monster, for example, is a "mystery". No-one has the faintest idea if it's there or what it is – and that's part of the attraction.'

'Yes . . .'

'Well, you want to turn your talk round so that everyone wrestles with the problem, realises there's no certain solution. I mean, you'd not expect one from that far back. They hadn't mastered writing then.'

'You mean, encourage debate rather than tell 'em the answer?'

'Exactly. Say, you could treat them as a jury. Identify half a

17

dozen possibilities, let them argue among themselves and then take a vote. Give them the sense that it's all open to doubt. Revel in the unknown.'

Richard's imagination was stirred. This sounded a better way to handle the Homers of the future.

He turned to his mentor. 'I might apply to Edinburgh one day. Which department did you say you were in?'

The woman smiled. 'I carefully didn't. It's not good to lie.'

'What d'you mean?'

'Well, I am a Professor at Cornell; and I'm here visiting Edinburgh. The way I combined the two may have been a little misleading – not least to Homer.

'But even today's facts are confusing. We can't possibly know what happened five thousand years ago. One of your many theories has to be true. Rejoice that we don't know which.'

Part of the Neolithic village of Skara Brae on the Orkneys

3.   CONNIE THE CONTORTIONIST

It had been a long day. I was an off duty WPC, on my way home from the Police Station when I decided to detour via my favourite pub in Stonegate, "The Grapes". It was York Performance Festival's first year and there had been plenty of teething problems, both inside the various venues and on the streets. The Council now had the venues under control but the street theatre was a bit random.

And that was when I had my second sighting of Connie.

The girl was coming down Stonegate on a unicycle. Nothing odd with that, except that she had a huge holdall balanced on her head as she pedalled.

I had interviewed Connie earlier, along with a host of other female street artists. There had been a spate of pick pocketing reported by the audience at the various sketches around the City; my Inspector had told me to look for any signs of the performers being accessories.

Connie was from Moldova and was, apparently, on her own. Her English was adequate but her key skill, she said, was being a contortionist. 'I learned ze skills from my parents,' she told me. 'Zey used to work in a circus.'

She had seemed honest but rather on edge. She was vague on her home address, but I wasn't into immigration control on this occasion. I could hear plenty more waiting to be interviewed in the corridor outside.

I was off-duty now and stopped opposite the Grapes to see her perform. It was almost dusk but there were still plenty of people about. Stonegate is one of the oldest streets in York and not brilliantly lit. Connie dismounted and dropped her holdall, then propped her unicycle against the pub wall. The girl seemed larger than I'd remembered. Then I saw the reason: she was wearing ridiculously high heels and a thick brown coat.

She began her act and the crowd started to gather.

'Ladies and gentlemen, I vant to talk to you this evening about ze alternative methods of travel. The first thing is that you should alvays travel light.' So saying she slipped out of her thick coat and dropped it on the floor behind her. Underneath she was wearing a striking, cerise cocktail dress with a scoop neck and wide skirt, over a petite frame. This must be her performance gear. She hadn't looked as glamorous as this at the Police Station.

'Never use a trunk!' she continued. 'You just need a bag, yes? A holdall is more flexible than a suitcase.' So saying she stood back, wriggled inside her holdall and zipped it up.

Her voice came from within. 'But zis is too large. I could get my whole family in here.' The bag was unzipped and she stepped out again.

'If you are going to travel light, then ze bag must not be too large.'

Now she stooped and retrieved a smaller holdall that was nestling inside the first.

'This one, yes, it plenty large enough for me.' So saying, she stepped forward and somehow crammed herself into the smaller bag, finally closing the zip from the inside.

A muffled sound came from within. 'Please, can someone lift up the ze bag. See how light it is.'

An American in an outlandish check jacket stepped forward and seized the bag. It was heavier than he'd been expecting but he lifted it anyway, and then threw it to his companion for good measure. The trouble was, his friend was not so good at catching. He missed and it landed with a "thump" on the pavement. I winced: that must have hurt. But a few seconds later the girl undid the zip and scrambled out.

'No-one can travel far without a few bumps along ze way,' she observed, as she gave her elbows a hefty rub.

'You must have ze shortest route to where you want to go.' Then she looked up. Between two of the Tudor dwellings on Stonegate was a cross girder, an iron beam twenty foot above the street, with a festival star hanging in the middle. Connie clambered onto the unicycle and then reached for a drainpipe running up the Grapes wall.

Before anyone could intervene she had clambered up and was seated astride the girder.

'Sometimes ze way ahead may look narrow,' she remarked. One by one she kicked off her shoes. Then hauled herself to her bare feet and started walking slowly across to the other side.

There was silence in the crowd, which had grown larger now. This was more dramatic than the living statues or the jugglers at the far end of Stonegate. The girder was only a couple of inches wide and there was nothing below but hard cobbles. If the girl fell she could do herself serious damage.

But I had a different concern. With every eye on the girl high above, her skirt billowing in the breeze, there would be a lack of guard on handbags, wallets and money belts down below. I turned to watch the crowd carefully. In the gloom it was hard to be sure but there seemed to be one man, in dark clothes and a bowler hat, moving around between them.

Connie finally reached the far side and grabbed another drainpipe. There was a round of applause as she shinned back to street level.

'You see, ladies and gentlemen, that however narrow ze path there is always a way. But you must travel light.' So saying she picked up the small holdall and pulled a smaller one from within. 'If you don't have much clothing a small bag is perfectly adequate.'

So saying, she prised herself, limb by limb, inside the latest bag and, with some effort, managed to pull the zip. The crowd was silent as the bag shook about on the pavement for a couple of minutes.

Then the zip was undone again and Connie emerged. This time she had discarded her cocktail dress and was dressed only in purple underwear.

A murmur of surprise and then another round of applause.

'I will demonstrate crossing ze street one more time. Zis time I need someone brave to act as my anchor,' she announced. 'Someone tall, strong and fit, yes, with a good head for heights.'

There was a moment's pause and then a human beanpole stepped forward.

'Thank you, sir,' said Connie. 'This time I will hang down from the girder by my arms. Once I am up I want you to clamber onto ze cycle and reach up to my ankles, then hold on to my feet as I go across. The journey will take perhaps five minutes. It will be hard work for both of us - but you will be only six or seven foot from the ground.'

The man had a moment of doubt and then agreed. It happened that he taught physical education. With the crowd watching it was hard to refuse the scantily clad girl. I guess he calculated that he would only be taking his own weight whereas Connie would have both of them hanging on her arms.

It took a few moments to arrange but the crowd was gripped.

Finally the pair set off, Connie holding the girder and the beanpole, who had been persuaded to remove a heavy jacket, holding her legs tightly. For her to make progress she had to move each hand in turn. The strain on the static arm as she did this looked immense.

Contrived or not, this was another opportunity for pick pockets. I turned my attention to the crowd. It was darker in the street now: dusk was almost upon us. Again I was aware of a dark-clothed man moving round at the rear. I slid behind to watch him more carefully but he seemed to disappear.

I glanced up. Connie was struggling now, breathing heavily, her face bright red. The beanpole was much heavier than she was but had not let go. Even so, she forced herself to complete the last few feet.

Someone had thoughtfully moved the unicycle over to the other side so the beanpole had somewhere to put his feet. Then it was all over. The man reached the cycle and slithered down, Connie, no longer holding his weight, reached the drain pipe and swarmed down after him.

She seized her companion's hand and gave a little bow to the crowd, to a generous round of applause.

'In an emergency you can travel with no clothing at all.' Once more Connie reached into the smaller bag and produced a bag that was smaller still. She set it in front of her; and then somehow managed to squeeze herself into it and closed the zip. There were more bumps and jolts.

No-one in the crowd was leaving now. Did she really mean . . .? Someone produced a camera and lined it up ready for her expected appearance. He took a trial picture and there was a bright flash, which for a few seconds stopped the crowd from seeing anything.

Then a sound came from the bag. 'Ze zip is jammed. I can't get out.'

There was a general murmur of disappointment.

After a few seconds a dark clothed man emerged from the crowd.

'Ladies and gentlemen, Connie seems to have hit a glitch in her equipment. So that's the end of the show. Please can we give her a big hand. And if you'd like to make a financial contribution please put it in this hat.'

A solid round of applause and then, slightly disappointed, the crowd started to drift away. The dark clothed man finished collecting and started to pull the bags and clothing together.

Was this the heart of the scam? A pretty girl doing a slow striptease, aided by aerial antics, while her partner fleeced the crowd? But if anyone had the pickings on them it must be the partner. I moved towards him.

'Sir, I am a police officer. We are concerned about the level of pick pocketing going on at street events. Would you come with me, please, to the local Police Station.'

'If you insist. But I protest my innocence. And what about Connie?'

'Leave her. She'll still be here on your return.' I used my mobile to ask for the nearest CCTV camera to be focussed on the smallest bag, which was lying beside the pub wall.

There was a special Police Station at the end of Stonegate during the Festival which we reached in a couple of minutes. But it was a waste of time. Even though the man was strip searched by one of my male colleagues there was nothing suspicious on him at all.

'Sorry sir, we have to take precautions,' I remarked as we headed back up Stonegate. It looked just as we had left it ten minutes earlier. I did a quick check with my CCTV contact: no, the bag had not moved at all.

'I'd better let Connie out,' he remarked. He bent down to tackle the errant zip.

I sensed something was going on but I had no idea what.

At last he managed to pull open the zip and peer inside.

'What the heck . . .?' he asked. He looked gobsmacked.

I lent forwards and looked inside. The bag was completely empty. Connie had claimed her prime skill was as a contortionist; but her real skill was as a disappearing act, getting away from us all.

It was only much later, after I finally got my glass of white wine in the Grapes, that I worked out what must have happened.

The Eureka moment came when the landlord announced that he would need to change the barrel. When he returned I caught his attention. 'As a matter of interest, where does the brewery unload its new barrels?'

'Out the front,' he replied. 'Didn't you see the access hatch in the pavement?'

And then the penny dropped. Connie hadn't been stumped by the zip, she had already disappeared down through the hatch into the pub cellar. The flash light which dazzled us had come, accidentally or otherwise, at just the right moment. The voice of complaint about the zip must have come from a voice recorder hidden in the bag.

Connie had been performing at this spot for almost a week, retiring to the pub ladies toilet to replace her clothing. No doubt she had had regular mugs of coffee to warm herself up on the way back, and had gained the confidence of the landlord. But I doubted he would talk to me.

'Moldova,' she had claimed. I started to wonder how she had reached the UK. In particular, what was the role of the dark-coated minder?

It came to me that he was not a pick pocket at all. No, he was a people smuggler, keeping close watch on Connie, trying to control his cargo until the fare for her trafficking had been fully paid.

To put it bluntly, was Connie getting away from me or was she escaping from her minder? I feared it was the latter. And to be honest, I was entirely behind her. I wouldn't try too hard to find out where she had gone.

Pedestrians enjoy Stonegate in the City of York. The girder over the street near the Olde Starre Inne can just be seen on the left. There is no street theatre on this occasion.

4. THE GRAVE BEYOND

The clanger marking the end of the shift had just sounded when Harry crept up on me along the narrow, uneven passage. Harry was a fellow-worker at the Levant Tin Mine; we were working out to sea, under the pounding Atlantic. There was no-one else labouring nearby. I'd been hammering tiny ingots of tin from a rough granite wall for eight hours and I was done.

'You and me, we've got things to sort out over my Hilda,' he began. Except for my fading headlamp it was pitch dark but I could just see Harry's eyes gleaming: he looked wild – almost insane. He was a giant of a man and he'd an ingot hammer of his own. Even a slow thinker like me could sense trouble.

'Hilda's an eye-catching woman,' I replied, trying to be diplomatic.

'As I'm sure you know. With all that time you've been spending together.'

'We're both in the St Just Choir, Harry. You could join too.'

'Singing's an activity for wimps. Trouble is, my Hilda comes home so late. As do you, Fred Trelawney. I was round at your place last night to check.'

That was a shock; but, then, I lived alone, now my Vera had gone. Earlier in 1919 the Spanish Flu had taken her. It was true Hilda had given me some comfort in the aftermath. But I swear: nothing had happened between us for Harry to get worked up

28

about.

I was about to remonstrate when I saw his anger was extending beyond words. In the gloom I sensed, rather than saw, his masonry hammer racing towards me.

It should have been the end. Would have been – except for the chunk of rock hanging from the passage roof. I knew it was there: I'd been working round it for hours. But Harry didn't.

His hammer caught it, ricocheted back and hit him hard in the face.

'Ahhh,' he screamed, staggering backwards in distress.

Then he tripped over my barrow, fell and cracked his head on the hard rock wall.

And lay completely still.

Looking back, I suppose I should have checked he was alright. He'd gone down with a real bang. But I wasn't inclined to take the risk. Much better, I thought, to get out while I had the chance.

My workplace was the furthest from the bottom of the main shaft. My quarrel with Harry meant I was starting back later than my shift-mates. But I knew better than to try and hurry. Lighting at the end of the mine was non-existent; it would be easy to get lost in the tangle of passageways, hewn by driven men in desperate pursuit of tin.

Every so often I stopped to listen: was there any sign Harry was coming after me? But I could hear nothing. The demented man must have been out cold.

Then, suddenly, I could hear a voice. It wasn't Harry: it sounded like a woman's – in fact it sounded like Vera's. I couldn't make out what it was saying but the tone was reassuring.

Was this a "Knocker", as I'd heard the older miners talk about? Help from the world beyond? If it was, the timing was priceless.

I'd been starting to feel guilty – maybe I had spent too long with Hilda, kept her away from Harry? Now the voice gave me a fresh perspective. After all, it was Harry that had been violent, not me.

I wondered what would happen when I reached the surface. Would it be better to tell the whole story to management - or to say nothing at all?

But if I told them, would they believe me? Harry was huge. I'd never have beaten him in a straight fight. How likely was it that he would have injured himself while trying to hurt me? I couldn't possibly prove what had really happened - could hardly believe it myself.

And what should I say about my friendship with his wife? Did I need to say anything? Had anyone seen me with Hilda on the weekly walks back from St Just? Had our detours, to keep us away from the rest of the choir and give us some privacy as we talked, been noticed? Had they been misinterpreted?

The more I pondered the worse it seemed to get.

Suddenly I heard louder voices. These weren't Knockers: Knockers didn't scream. These sounded like men ahead of me in desperate trouble. Something must have happened at the shaft bottom. Steadily I plodded on - what else had gone wrong on this fateful shift?

And then I came to the bottom of the main shaft: it was mayhem.

I only had my almost extinct headlight so it took a while to make sense of it. There was a huge muddle of machinery. Normally we miners would expect to make our way back to the surface via the "Man Engine". Two sets of ladders, attached either side of a huge wheel on the surface, rotated by a steam engine. The ladders oscillated up and down for twelve foot. You'd to stand on one ladder as it pulled up, then transfer to the second as it reached its peak, so you'd be scooped steadily upwards. Transferring back and forth, twelve foot up each time, a miner could reach the top in twenty minutes – faster than the toiling hour it took in the old days.

But something cataclysmic must have happened to the Engine. The wreckage - yards and yards of smashed ladders - lay at the foot of the shaft.

And as I looked harder, I saw that there must have been men on the ladders as the crash occurred – there were half a dozen dead or dying bodies lying amidst the broken equipment.

With a shock I realised that, but for my encounter with Harry, I would have been among them.

There was nothing I could down here. Fortunately I'd worked in the mine before the Man Engine arrived so I knew there was an old way out. I almost panicked – I could only hope the Knockers might help me find it. It was a struggle but, eventually, I found the old stairway and started on my way to the surface.

My worries on accounting for Harry started to fade. Much bigger problems faced the mine now.

At last I reached the surface. Great shouts of joy from the distraught crowd!

I explained I'd been late reaching the Man Engine and so had escaped the great disaster. I reported the six bodies I'd seen at the bottom. Now, though, the biggest challenge was part-way down, where it was believed many more men, riding the ladder during the crash, were still alive.

It took days to reach and rescue them and many died in the meantime. In the end over thirty miners died in the accident – one of the worst in all Cornwall.

So what happened over Harry? Well, maybe the Knockers were right to encourage me. After the mine shaft had been restored, it was decided to abandon the lowest level of working. So for many years no-one knew Harry's body was down there. He was just written off as another casualty of the disaster.

But there was an upside. Hilda and I married a few months later.

Present-day remains of Levant Tin Mine on the north coast of the Lands End Peninsular

5. VINTAGE FRIENDSHIP

I stood in the foyer of the London Museum, heart pounding. Sally and I had not met face to face for a quarter of a century. A scrawled email on her Christmas card had led to this planned reunion. I'd never been to the London Museum but Sally had some connection or other so it seemed a fine place to meet.

Eleven o'clock, we'd agreed. I was there early – not through desperation, simply London Transport being unexpectedly efficient. I was astounded by the size of the foyer. There were dozens of people wandering about, although not many children: Sally had been wise enough to avoid us meeting in the half-term holiday.

My friend was not so early. A London girl, she'd got travelling down to a fine art years ago. A man can expect to be kept waiting. Though this was no wedding, just two old work colleagues renewing contact.

Would I recognise her? We'd not thought to exchange photos, the question hadn't crossed my mind. But twenty five years was a long time. I didn't know Sally's exact age but she must be well into her fifties. No doubt she was still fun to be with, but what colour was her hair? It used to be dark brown - we'd known each other a long time ago - but now it might be anything from amber to silver grey.

Unless she had changed a great deal she would still look elegant but I had no idea what she'd be wearing.

Five past eleven. No sign of Sally, though I noticed several intelligent, middle-class women wandered about. A horrible thought struck me. If I'd find it hard to recognise her, how hard was it for her to know me? My once ginger hair was now grey and where once I'd been slim I now possessed an ample paunch.

Was she having as much trouble spotting me as I was finding her?

Ten past eleven. I'd already circulated the foyer three times. I was back at the cafe, about to treat myself to a cup of coffee, when I was tapped lightly on the shoulder. I turned to see an attractive, middle-aged woman, sporting a cheerful smile.

'Sally,' I exclaimed, 'great to see you - after all these years.'

She seemed almost as surprised to see me and gave me a generous hug.

'Should we do coffee first?' she suggested. 'I'll buy, you grab a table. Do you still take sugar?'

'I never did, Sally. An Americano will be fine.'

I grabbed a table and watched her in the queue, as bubbly as ever. Not as slim as I'd remembered, but men weren't the only ones who could gain weight.

Soon she returned with the coffees to our table.

We peeled off our coats. Sally's sheer cream blouse revealed more than I remembered from two decades ago. Concentrate, I thought, on her face.

'Do you remember that awful coffee in the Coal Board canteen?' I asked.

'It was supposed to be tea,' she protested. 'Anyway, what are you doing now?'

'I'm retired,' I replied. 'These days I write horror stories.'

She laughed. 'So you learned something from the Coal Board?'

I was tempted to reminisce but I'd resolved to start with the present. I wanted friendship now, not just to explore memory lane.

'I've brought you my latest book,' I said, as I extracted a paperback.

She took it with interest. 'Thank you. That's very kind. So no pen name?'

I shrugged. 'No-one knows me anyway.'

She skimmed the back page then flipped inside for the potted biography.

'Must keep you busy, Peter. So how many have you written now?'

'This is the fifth. They're getting sharper. It's taken me a decade to get the hang of it.' This was my favourite topic of conversation; I mustn't talk too much.

'Anyway, what do you do, Sally?'

'I'm retired too. My hobby is historical archives. That's why I suggested meeting here. This month they've got a special display of the Magna Carta. I'm afraid that's the bit they charge for.'

'Well, we've got our pensions – till the next financial meltdown, anyway. It may give me material for a new story.'

As I piled our cups on the tray she glanced at her watch. 'Time for the Magna Carta I think.' We gathered our belongings and headed for the payment desk.

The Magna Carta Exhibition celebrated eight hundred years since the document had been signed. The entry price was high, so the crowds in there were much smaller.

It started with displays about life in the Middle Ages, the role of the King and the power of the Barons. Then came Runnymede. The culmination was a display, in a glass case and a darkened room, of the precious document itself.

Sally and I had talked only occasionally. She'd asked me to act as her photographer, using her camera to capture her in front of the various displays. There were warnings not to use flash but none banning photographs altogether.

Security was unobtrusive. I didn't see anyone in uniform; they must rely on hidden cameras. Since Sally's coat was still in her rucksack and her blouse translucent, the pictures were certainly glamorous. Other visitors probably thought I was with a film star.

By the time we'd reached the document room it was midday. I noticed there was no-one else in there.

'Do you want a close-up of the Magna Carta?' I asked.

'Please. But you might not want me on this one.'

At least the girl was aware she was a distraction.

'You'll have to use flash this time,' she observed, and showed me how to turn it on.

I took some time to position myself high over the display case, taking care I had the priceless document in focus. Sally had stood somewhere off to the side.

I was just pressing the camera button when two things happened. First there was a loud crack from somewhere to my left. At the same time all the diffused lighting went off.

In the ensuing darkness the flash from the camera burnt into my eyes; for a few seconds I could see nothing at all.

Confused, I stepped gingerly back from the display case,

rubbing my eyes. There was a glimmer of light reaching the room from the Runnymede display next door.

I kept rubbing and gradually my eyesight was restored.

But where was Sally? That cream blouse was practically fluorescent. If anything could be seen in here it should be her - unless she'd taken it off. I squinted round the room but she was no longer there.

I was, though, no longer alone. Two uniformed security men had appeared, one armed with a powerful torch. 'Stay still please, sir,' he commanded.

Then he pointed his torch at the display cabinet. To my horror I saw that the sliding window at the side of the case, where Sally had been standing, was no longer closed. And the precious document, the starting point for the rule of law and habeas corpus in the western world, had been scooped up from its ornate cushion and was no longer inside.

An hour later I was still with the two security men but now in their control room. A bank of monitors, linked to security cameras, showed various points in the Museum. The Magna Carta display room was one of them, though, sadly, it was now closed to visitors.

The senior man turned to me. 'So you met this woman for the first time in the café?'

'That's right,' I replied. 'For a few seconds I thought she was my old friend Sally. As soon as she brought the coffees and we started talking I realised I'd made a dreadful mistake. The odd thing was that the woman was playing the game too. I mean, she can't possibly have really been called Sally, she just picked up the

37

name I first used.'

'We've been watching her for a couple of weeks, sir. Every day she's come into the Magna Carta room with a different man, but they're always holding the same camera.'

'I can explain that,' I interrupted. 'She asked me to photographer her and lent me her camera to do so.'

'Yes. Our guess is that she approaches single middle-aged men in the foyer and asks them some question along the lines of, "Are you my Internet date?"'

'She's always wearing a revealing top,' he continued, 'so, if they're on their own, quite a few will say yes. You broke the pattern, sir, in that you claimed to recognise her.'

'Is she mad?'

'Completely sane, sir. She gets to the display room precisely at midday, which is when the security shifts change. What she can't control is the crowd numbers in the Magna Carta room at that time.'

'There was no-one else there today,' I remembered.

'For her trick it had to be empty so she could flip the lights just as she forced the lock and grabbed the document. The flash on the camera gave her a few seconds and that was enough. Time enough, anyway, for her to slip on her coat and disappear before we could get there.'

'So I just had to provide the flash?'

'And then to be the fall guy, distracting us for a few moments.'

I thought for a moment.

'But if you already suspected her, why didn't you arrest her earlier?'

38

'Until she took the document she'd not broken any law, sir. But after her third dead-on-noon appearance we took the precaution of setting one of our colleagues to follow her so we knew where she lived. She went there again straight after the incident; should be back any minute.'

Just at that moment the door opened and a middle aged woman came in. She was elegantly slim, with long, silver-grey hair.

She saw me and exclaimed, 'Peter!'

'Sally.' I gave her a determined hug. At last I'd reunited with my old colleague – and this one was the genuine article.

'It worked, guys,' she announced. 'Our glamorous villain gave me back the document. I decided that retrieving the Magna Carta was more important than the two of us fighting over it. It would be rather a shame if it came back torn in two.'

She turned to me. 'Thank you, Peter, for playing along, knowingly or otherwise. Now we can really explore the Museum. By the way, did you bring me a copy of your new book?'

The London Museum does a tremendous job bringing history to life for Londoners. Its displays cover aspects of life from Roman times to the present day. As far as I know it has never hosted a Magna Carta exhibition.

6. TOAST

Until today it had been a fabulous sabbatical. Day after day the sun had beamed down on Scotland's North-west Highlands, with wave after wave of awesome scenery. The drive had done at least something to suspend my loneliness and the sense of self-pity that rarely left me as a recently-bereaved doctor.

But this morning it had started to rain, three normal weeks of precipitation in a few hours. I had struggled to navigate the single-track back road to Lochinver, seeing almost nothing through a rain-engulfed windscreen. At times – most of all when I met a motor home on a one-in-four slope at a hairpin bend - I thought I might never make it. Speed was a delusion and now darkness was not far away.

Then I'd seen the magic sign, "Bed and Breakfast: Vacancies" outside the cottage ahead.

It was late October. In my misery I'd made no effort to book accommodation ahead so there was no smart guest-house in Lochinver awaiting my arrival. But this might do. There was already one car in the narrow drive.

I parked behind it, unfolded myself, wrapped my cagoule tightly to keep out at least some of the rain and squelched over to the porch.

'I hadn't expected visitors in weather like this but yes, I can offer you a room for the night,' said the small, wiry man who came to the door after longer delay than I would have liked. 'Do come in. My name's Cameron. Would you like a cup of tea and some shortbread?' I spotted a certificate on the wall: this five-star accommodation was owned by Cameron and Eleanor McKenzie. As I wiped the rain from my spectacles and peered around I saw I had chosen well. It might be off the beaten track but it was a top quality guest-house.

A couple of hours later I had had a long, hot shower, changed into dry clothes and settled down to watch international football in the lounge. It seemed I was the only guest. If it had been fine I would have gone on to find food but Cameron told me the nearest place offering anything remotely edible was six miles away. I'd done enough mechanised surfing on soggy roads for one day.

Cameron added that Eleanor could cook me a light meal for a small extra charge. I accepted and supplemented the piping-hot spaghetti Bolognese which later appeared with some wine I'd bought in Durness. Cameron shared a glass with me: he wasn't going anywhere on a night like this.

The football was disappointing but England had a new manager so no surprise there. Cameron and I finished the bottle and with highland courtesy he fetched another from the kitchen to see us through the extra time. Generously, he made sure I had the larger share.

I was pleasantly befuddled by the time I headed for bed and slept like the proverbial log.

Next morning I sat down for what would have been a full English breakfast except that I was in Scotland. Cameron was being waiter and I assumed Eleanor had the production role in the kitchen. I was alone in the dining room.

I had ample coffee but I saw, as I stared at the bacon, sausage and eggs, that he'd forgotten the toast. I waited for a minute but there was no sign of life. I gave a call but it wasn't heeded. So I headed for what I assumed must be the kitchen.

Cameron was surprised to see me, said he'd bring the toast along shortly. As I returned to the dining room it occurred to me that he had been there on his own. So where was Eleanor?

It was a question I put to him when he brought in the toast. He looked slightly uncomfortable and mumbled something as I took a scoop of highland marmalade, then shot back to the kitchen. As I tucked in to my breakfast I pondered. It was none of my business but I was intrigued. Cameron had spoken several times of Eleanor but I had yet to see her in person.

Did she really exist or was she a figment of his imagination? Was she someone he'd invented to make single guests like myself feel more at ease in this remote household? No, that didn't fit with the names on the five-star certificate.

Maybe she was ill upstairs – perhaps, like me, she had a hangover? The next time Cameron appeared I told him that I was a medical doctor: was there anything I could do for Eleanor before I went on my way?

He looked irritated. No, there was nothing. But he went no further to explain her absence.

This was one mystery I wasn't intended to solve. I shrugged my shoulders, packed my bag and went on my way. The rain had stopped and the remote scenery looked as stunning as ever.

But to my surprise the track I had been following only went another mile and then petered out beside a rocky shoreline. It was quiet and picturesque but I tested the temperature: it was nowhere near warm enough for a swim.

I consulted my map. I must have gone off my intended route in the gloom of the evening before. There was no choice but to retrace my tracks. As I went past my guest-house I saw that there was no longer a car in the drive. I deduced Cameron must have set out soon after me, heading in the opposite direction.

Perhaps he was on his way to visit Eleanor in hospital, though that would be a long drive. The nearest one would be Inverness – and that would be three hours away. Poor chap. I wasn't the only one with problems.

As I came over the brow of the one-in-four hill I'd struggled with the day before, I saw what looked like an accident down below. It was a car the same colour as the one I'd seen parked at my guesthouse. There was no other traffic about so I guessed it must be Cameron's.

He'd probably been driving too fast on the steep, slippery track and failed to take account of the hairpin. It looked serious: the car was well off the road and had smashed into the rocks nearby.

My self-pity seemed an indulgence as I saw a fresh tragedy ahead of me. I drove very carefully down to see what I could do to help and parked where the car had gone off the road. Then I grabbed my medical bag and struggled through the gorse to the wrecked car.

But I could see, as I wrenched open the door, that poor Cameron was beyond medical help. His neck was broken, his breathing had ceased and a check on his pulse showed his heart was no longer beating.

My mobile phone did not work in this remote corner of the

Highlands. It hardly mattered; I knew that even if I could summon an air ambulance to take him to Inverness it would be too late.

But the death still needed to be reported: this was a police matter. There was no choice but to drive to the nearest village and make use of a land-line. I would be visiting Lochinver after all.

As I continued my journey, taking more care than the day before – I was pretty shaken by what I'd seen – I noticed another car coming towards me. I pulled into the next passing place and flagged it down. A woman was driving with a man seated beside her.

'I'd better warn you,' I said, 'there's been an accident ahead. A car came down that steep hill too fast and went off the road at the hairpin. The vehicle's a write-off and I'm afraid the driver is dead. I'm a doctor so I know there's nothing we can do. I'm on my way to report it in Lochinver.'

The pair looked shocked.

'Which way was he travelling?' asked the man.

'The same way as me. In fact I'd stayed at his guest-house last night. I left before him but I went the wrong way, so he ended up ahead of me.'

There was a pause. I noticed the couple were looking at one another.

'But there's only one cottage along this road.' The woman sounded anxious. 'And that's our guest-house.'

I looked at her, bemused. Then cogs started to whir. 'Are you by chance Eleanor McKenzie?'

'Yes, and this is my husband Cameron. We should have been

at home but we had a call yesterday afternoon to say one of my relatives in Durness had been taken ill. But when we got there it was a false alarm. No-one admitted making the call. We've been trying to make sense of it all the way back.'

'So the man who acted as my host wasn't Cameron at all. But why should he pretend to me that he was?'

The real Cameron had been thinking hard. 'Our guest-house has a very narrow drive. Once you'd driven in there, he wouldn't be able to drive out till you'd gone again. Pretending to be the host for the night would be a low-hassle way of seeing you off without drawing attention to himself. No-one else would know you'd been there. Did you leave any trace of your identity?'

I thought for a moment. 'Well, he asked me for payment in cash. I'd have been suspicious but that's happened to me several times in these parts so I didn't think much of it. And I certainly wasn't given chance to sign any visitor's book. I looked for one, in fact, but it had disappeared. If I hadn't seen his crashed car or met you I'd have been miles away.'

Later, after we had summoned the police, the crashed car was found to be full of valuables owned by Cameron and Eleanor. And Cameron recognised the dead man: he'd been a guest with them the previous week. No wonder he'd known how their guest-house functioned.

In truth I hadn't contributed much to the recovery of the treasures but the couple did invite me to stay a couple more nights, without charge, while the police completed their enquiries.

It was an odd cure for self-pity but it helped me a lot.

The majestic Suilven, a few miles from Lochinver.

7. A HEART OF GOLD

The passion of Laurie and Greg for golf was legendary; and matched only by their inability to play the game with any deep skill. Every Monday evening, from April until October, they would be found hacking their way round the Dog, a golf course in rural Oxfordshire well-tuned to their limited capabilities. In the winter months they would spend time reading golfing magazines and occasionally buy new clubs – items which, each assured the other, would make all the difference next season.

There was not much between them in their ability to complete a round. Laurie would hit the ball hard and high but not necessarily towards the flag. He tended to tack his way round the course, navigating from one side of the fairway to the other. The main cost of playing golf for him was the number of balls he lost in the long grass or bushes along the way. Once or twice he had had to stop a round early as he'd used all the spare balls he brought with him, plus all those of his playing partner.

By contrast Greg was a plodder. He generally hit the ball straight. It trundled along the fairway but as it rarely achieved takeoff it did not go very far. Greg regarded it as a success to reach the green in single figures.

Once the two had reached the green it was largely a matter of luck. The Dog was not over-visited and survived financially by sparse maintenance. The greens were unwatered (except by rain)

47

and had a few bare patches, so even a skilful player might struggle. Laurie often asserted, after yet another putt deviated from the hole, that, 'The early Tiger Woods would have struggled to make par here.' It was a consoling remark even if probably untrue.

No-one famous had ever played at the Dog, or ever would.

Which of Laurie or Greg won a particular round depended on whose limitations were the more serious on the day. Each played to win; but their friendship was based on a common love of the game rather than a need to beat the other at all costs. The round would always finish with pints of Brakspear and empathetic reconstruction of their latest rounds. Several shots would be scooped from each score by the end of the evening.

It was one May evening that the pair first came across Maeve O'Riordon as they wrestled with the second hole. Maeve was on a path beside the fairway, accompanied by a golden retriever and a bloodhound. Both dogs had a great deal more energy than she did and Laurie feared that one or other would make off with his ball - which would be a pity, as for once he'd hit a shot onto the fairway. He was about to remonstrate then realised the old lady might not approve of raw Anglo-Saxon.

Greg was closer to her and saw the need to intervene more gently.

'Hello. Laurie and I play here every Monday. Are these your dogs?'

'Oh, hello. I'm Maeve.' Greg detected a strong Irish accent. 'I live over there.' She waved inconclusively at a tumbledown cottage in the distance. 'No, I started to walk them for a neighbour who had a stroke. I hadn't realised till I saw you two with your clubs that this was a live golf course. Ridiculous, isn't it? And I've lived around here for thirty years.'

Greg saw that his partner had managed to keep both dogs from running off with his ball and was about to play his next shot. Laurie wasn't used to animals – it wouldn't look good to hit either of them; and in any case two accurate shots in a row was, for him, almost impossible. The ball flew into the air and landed in a nearby bush.

'Begorrah, you lads like the scenic route,' said the woman. 'Can my dogs help you find it?'

She gave a whistle and both dogs disappeared into the bushes and returned, each with a golf ball in their mouths.

As Laurie bent to see which one was his, the dogs ran off again and returned with two more. By the time Greg and Maeve had reached him they had assembled over a dozen.

Introductions were made and an unusual friendship began.

From now on they came across Maeve regularly on Monday evenings. Greg suspected that she timed her dog-walk to make sure they met. Even when she had no dogs she was still there. She was obviously lonely; and had an unexpected interest in golf.

In some ways Maeve was like them: a genuine fan with almost no real understanding of detail. She would praise their efforts without any hint of criticism.

One day Laurie saw her, as he drove up towards the Dog, coming out of a smart thatched house in the village. He was pleased to see evidence that she was flourishing. It would have been sad if she was surviving her twilight days on food banks.

Then, for a few weeks, they did not meet her at all. They

assumed she'd gone off on holiday but as the weeks went by they started to wonder.

Then one day there was a postcard waiting at the Dog reception.

'Dear Laurie and Greg,' they read. 'I don't know your addresses so this is the only way I can get in touch. I'm sorry to say I'm in the Nuffield Ward at the Royal Berks, recovering from a stroke. If either of you had a moment, it would be lovely to see you.'

The card was signed, 'Your fellow golf lover, Maeve.'

Sad news. The men quickly identified two evenings later in the week when one or other could drop in at the hospital, but agreed they must not stay long.

Their subsequent game of golf was rather a depressed affair and neither felt like a drink afterward.

Laurie had the first date. It took a while to find the ward and he was shocked when he saw Maeve at the far end. She had no visitors and not a single Get Well card by her bedside. Lying flat on her back, she looked extremely frail.

However, the sight of her golfing friend seemed to buck her up. 'Laurie!' she exclaimed. 'By all that's wonderful. You got my message then. It's so good to see you.'

'Maeve,' he smiled. 'I brought you some flowers. Greg is coming tomorrow with the grapes. We were so sad to hear about this. We'd no idea – thought you might be on holiday.'

'I wish,' she said, her eyes filling with tears. 'No, I'm here all on my own.'

'Do you have any relatives? Is there anyone you'd like me to get in touch with?'

Maeve took a moment to collect her thoughts.

'There's not many, Laurie, they're all in western Ireland. And I haven't seen them for so long. That's a way to come for anyone to visit an old lady.'

'Well, what about local friends? Say the woman who owned the dogs you walked when we first met?'

'She died, young man. "Complications", they said. I hope I've not got the same thing.'

Laurie gave up at this point and started telling her about his latest golfing disaster. But after twenty minutes he saw her eyes were starting to close.

'Maybe that's enough for now, Maeve. Don't worry, Greg and I will keep visiting you anyway.'

Greg was equally distressed when he saw Maeve the next day. Afterwards he rang Laurie.

'She's very ill, isn't she? I managed to talk to the Ward Nurse on the way out, implied I was one of her nephews. She thinks you're the other, by the way. Reading between the lines, the nurse was very pessimistic about her chances. I fear she may not be with us much longer.'

Both men had commitments that took them away that week-end so neither could visit the hospital again. Greg managed to get through to the ward on the phone before he left and learned that Maeve was "still hanging on". It was not a promising prognosis. Monday's golf would have the air of a wake.

But when they met in the Dog reception that evening there was

51

someone else waiting for them, a smart-looking man in a business suit. 'Now, am I right that you two are Laurie and Greg?' The two concurred.

'My name is Paddy O'Riordan,' he continued. 'I'm a distant relative of Maeve. I only heard on Friday that she was ill. I came at once, fortunately just in time. We had a good chat on Saturday evening. By yesterday, I'm afraid, she was unconscious. And then . . .'

He saw the surprise on their faces. 'Have you not been told? Maeve passed away early this morning.'

There was a moment's silence.

'She was a fine old lady,' said Laurie.

'A real golfing enthusiast,' added Greg. 'Thank you for coming out here to tell us in person.'

Paddy acknowledged his words. 'But I'm not just here for that. Did Maeve not tell you about her bequest?' The two shook their heads.

'She said you two needed encouragement to play in the right way. So she wanted you to play a match with me as the referee. I was to pick the winner and they would receive a small legacy. I have to fly home later this week so could we do that this evening?'

After the news neither man felt much like playing golf but it was something Maeve had requested. Ten minutes later, both rather shaken, they stood on the first tee with Paddy beside them.

Greg would play the same way whatever the context. Soon he was hacking down the fairway, heading for the flag.

But Laurie found himself with conflicting emotions. Suddenly he recalled the smart house in the village he had seen Maeve

52

exiting. She was probably quite well off; and on her own admission had no close relatives. How large was this legacy? It might be well worth winning.

Laurie had no more residual golfing skill than Greg. But his style meant he spent longer off the fairways, away in the bushes. For the first time in his golfing life he was tempted to cheat.

After a high but off-line stroke his ball disappeared into the trees. He plunged after it until he was well out of sight. There was no chance of finding the ball but he had plenty of spares; and a good arm. The golfer seized the replacement and threw it as hard as he could towards the flag.

It turned out he was better at throwing than driving. Emerging from the bushes he saw that his ball had landed close to the green. Meanwhile Greg was still plodding his way up the fairway.

'Good shot,' his partner acknowledged. The referee made a note on his card.

So the first hole was Laurie's, by a four-shot margin. Which set the pattern for the rest of the round.

Finally the course was completed and the referee looked at his card. 'I hereby declare the winner of the Maeve O'Riordon Memorial Award to be . . . Greg.'

Both men looked incredulous.

'Sorry,' said Greg, 'You've added the scores up wrong. Laurie won most of the holes, surely?'

But Laurie knew he had not won fairly. As he thought about it he felt ashamed and deeply guilty.

'Greg, I'm so sorry. All my shots out of the bushes were thrown. I should have been disqualified many times over. Well done. You deserve to win.' He shook his hand warmly.

Paddy saw both men needed some explanation. He drew a deep breath.

'Maeve told me I was to pick the winner. But she didn't say it was on number of strokes. She asked me to count the acknowledgments made by each of you. And this evening Greg has been exceptionally generous and Laurie has been somewhat silent.'

The referee hunted in his bag and produced a small shield. 'I had this made up this afternoon with funds from Maeve. It's a Memorial Award, dated today:

"To the best golfer, not judged by fewest strokes but by generosity of heart. Assess the means and not the ends."'

'Do you know what lay behind this?' asked Greg, mystified.

'Well, she'd seen the result of excess competition in the life of her husband.'

'How d'you mean?'

'Did she not tell you? Her husband was Irish Amateur Champion one year in the 1970s. Next year he keeled over with a heart attack. When you look at this, remember his early death - and beware.'

8.   FIXED POINT IN A CRISIS

'I can't help it, Andrew, there's a gap somewhere in your logic. Leave me the draft and I'll have a look for it over the weekend.'

His visitor was about to remonstrate when there was a knock at the door.

Dr Peter McNeil glanced at his watch. 'Hell's bells, five o'clock already. I'm sorry Andrew, I've an undergraduate tutorial starting now. That'll be Miss Goody Two Shoes – she's always early.'

A Princeton lecturer, his friend understood the pressures of academic life. He started pulling together the pages of the disputed document, which was sprawled across the desk after their intense argument.

'Remember, Peter,' he warned, 'this is all hush, hush. I haven't told anyone I'm working on this. It's just that you're a world expert on elliptic functions and I was in Cambridge for the conference, so I thought I'd look you up. Thank you for your help. It's been really good to catch up.'

There was a second, louder knock at the door, slightly more impatient. The real world always impacted eventually, even on pure mathematicians.

McNeil sighed and headed to let his visitors in. Opening it, the two attendees for his pure maths tutorial were waiting outside – a small woman with bright eyes and dark, curly hair and a tall man, less alert, but with a flamboyant ginger beard.

'Come right in,' McNeil told them cheerfully.

He was about to introduce them to his distinguished visitor from the United States when it occurred to him that, if his friend wanted the visit kept secret, it was best to say nothing to anyone. Students were notorious disseminators of gossip and though these two would never have heard of him, word might reach others who had: his friend was, after all, the world's best Number Theorist.

But the man was obviously in a hurry to leave anyway and slid past them and down the stairs to the courtyard without another word.

George Goode swung her rucksack off her shoulder and sat at McNeil's desk, then scooped out an assortment of notes. Her fellow-student, Alastair Dunlop, flopped down beside her. The tutorial – the cornerstone of an Oxbridge education – was about to begin.

This was the point at which deficiencies in lectures – or, at least, in the ways the students had taken them in – could be ironed out by a seasoned academic. That was the theory, anyway.

'Today,' Dr McNeil told the pair, 'our subject is Fixed Point Theorems. Do you remember this from your Analytic Topology lectures?'

'It was mentioned, Dr McNeil,' responded George. 'But the whole thing seemed so obvious to Swinnerton Dyer that he didn't bother to unpack it.'

'He gave us an outline proof,' explained her colleague, 'but it stops five lines from the end. It was obvious to the lecturer how it would finish – but it wasn't clear to me. I'm afraid it's not the

56

first time that's happened.'

'Worst of all, he didn't give us any intuitive feel of what it means,' added George, looking wistful. To enjoy the maths she needed a practical sense of what was going on.

McNeil sighed. Swinnerton Dyer was outstandingly clever – he had won four chess "blues" playing for Oxford, then another four for Cambridge – but he did tend to assume his students were as clever as he was. In most cases that was a false assumption.

'I can help you there, anyway,' said McNeil. There was a pile of rough paper on his desk. He straightened it and seized the top sheet.

'Imagine that this is a sheet of graph paper and there's an identical one underneath. Now watch.'

Making sure he did not tear the sheet, he proceeded to crush it between his hands into an untidy, crumpled ball. This he placed carefully back on top of the pile.

'Now, Brouwer's Fixed Point Theorem asserts that under the transformation I've just done, there is at least one point on the crumpled sheet that is exactly on top of the same physical point on the sheet below.' He smiled at the students.

'In other words, however it was squashed, there's one point that hasn't been moved at all. Does that help you visualise the Fixed Point Theorem?'

George stared at the crumpled sheet: yes, that made some kind of sense. Certainly, it covered only a fraction of the sheet below. It was pretty likely that at least one point would be over the place where it began – but not certain. So the Theorem was saying something valuable.

Then she spotted a difficulty. 'But suppose that you hadn't

crumpled the sheet but you had folded it and then torn it in two. And after that you'd swapped the two sheets round and placed them back on the pile. The top half would now be over the bottom on the sheet beneath and the bottom over the top. Like this.'

She seized the sheet beneath, tore it in two and replaced it as she had described. 'There's no fixed point between the two sheets now, is there?'

McNeil looked pleased. 'Well done, George. That's why the Theorem is only true if the transformation is "compact".'

The tutorial continued on its way. McNeil helped the pair to complete the missing lines of the proof and the whole thing started to make sense. The sense of panic which had seized George since the end of the last topology lecture started to fade away.

An hour later, George walked out onto Trinity Great Court. A bitter, autumnal wind was blowing in, straight from the Urals. She hastened down Trinity Lane and back to her college, Trinity Hall, next door.

She was surprised to be called over to the desk as she walked through the Porters' Lodge.

'Miss Goode, Professor Körner asked you to call in on him straight away. He said it was very urgent.'

The professor was the senior mathematics tutor in her college. What on earth did he want?

A minute later she was knocking at Tom Körner's door and being invited in. There was no-one else present.

'Thank you, George, for coming so promptly. I had Dr

McNeil on the phone a few minutes ago,' Körner began. 'He sounded like a man in a panic. His previous visitor had just phoned him. He said he'd left one or two sheets of the paper they were discussing on McNeil's desk and now they've disappeared. Then McNeil remembered you'd had a pile of papers with you: did you by any chance scoop his sheet up with your own?'

'I don't think so,' replied George. 'But we can take a look.'

She swung the backpack off her shoulder, scooped out the muddle of notes inside and plonked them on Körner's desk. 'I presume what he's lost is typed on A4 paper?'

'I assume so. But McNeil said that some important scrawls had been added in their discussions - in green ink - about a potential bug. They should be easy to spot if they're here.'

For a few minutes the two thumbed through the various sets of notes. George had made a few bored doodles – impressions of her lecturers - but fortunately these were drawn in pencil and without the matching names were hard to recognise. There was no sign of anything in green.

'What about your fellow student?'

'Oh, Alastair just had a small notepad. He wouldn't have picked up anything.'

Körner noted the ambiguity with a smile. 'Mm. And – just to be clear - you came straight back here from the tutorial?'

There was no hint of accusation in the way he posed the question but George still felt an implicit challenge.

'Straight back here, Dr Körner. The tutorial finished in Great Court at 6:03. The wind was very cold so I was back here at the Porter's Lodge by 6:10. I walked fast and didn't meet anyone I knew on the way.'

Körner did not question her further. Her answer had left little more that could reasonably be asked.

There was a pause as both considered the problem.

'Is McNeil's problem the typed notes or the scrawls?' asked George. 'And why is it so important?'

'It must be the scrawls, I think, George. It would be easy enough for his visitor to run off more notes – unless he didn't want any duplicates to exist. McNeil told me his visitor's a Number Theorist – the poor bloke's probably still grappling with Fermat's Last Theorem.'

George remembered that this was a famous conjecture, made by a French mathematician in 1637, which was still waiting to be proved in 1989.

'If it's that secret, Dr Körner, might McNeil be hoping to imply the whole thing had been stolen – then, later, he could publish a correction under his own name?'

'One or two universities might behave like that, George, but I doubt anyone would do so here. I should think his visitor was just keen to get back the scrawls to fix his bug. The trouble is, McNeil had just enjoyed an exhausting tutorial with you two. He can't remember exactly what his previous ideas had been.'

George thought back again to the tutorial. When it began, McNeil's desk had been rather a mess – but presumably he'd examined everything on it carefully before ringing up Körner? He was an intelligent man, he must have done.

No, she'd no idea. It was a minor mystery but she'd no idea if it was important.

The solution came to George next morning. She was sitting at her desk, working on her next assignment, as the cleaner tidied her room and emptied her rubbish bin.

Emptied her rubbish bin . . . Eureka. She rushed down the stairs and over to Dr Körner's rooms; fortunately he was in.

'I know where it'll be,' she said, breathing hard. 'Tell him to look for the crumpled ball of paper in his waste paper basket – the one he used to help us understand the Fixed Point Theorem. I bet that's where the notes ended up.'

The professor seized his phone to contact McNeil. But would he manage to get through to him in time?

Or would an efficient cleaner, already at work, delay a major mathematical breakthrough?

George was on her way back to her room when she met Alastair in the Front Court.

McNeil had been scathing at the suggestion that he look in his wastepaper basket. 'I'm not an idiot, Tom. That was the first thing I did, before I rang anybody. It's certainly not there.'

Körner had been forced to beat a tactical retreat, after which George had left rather hurriedly.

'Hey, George,' asked Alastair, 'd'you remember tearing that sheet in two in the tutorial yesterday?'

'Yes?'

'Well, I found I'd put both halves into my notebook. They're here, covered in green scrawls. Might McNeil want them?'

'He probably does. I'll give them to Tom Körner straight away.' She seized them and turned back the way she had just come.

On such slender threads can academic progress stand or fall.

Professor Andrew Wiles worked on his own to find a proof of Fermat's Last Theorem from 1986 to 1993. His proof was first announced at a Cambridge maths conference but a mistake was later found. Another year of research was needed before the final solution emerged.

George Goode later married and became George Gilbert, business analyst and heroine of the "Cornish Conundrum" crime stories. You will meet her again later in this book.

The Front Court of Trinity Hall Cambridge, as photographed by the author in 1966. It hasn't changed much since, although women are now admitted as students.

9.   A HOLLOW MEMORIAL

Even for the Orkneys it was a ferocious storm. He was glad he wouldn't be putting to sea again tonight.

Archie Macleod had just secured his boat in the Sand Geo, near the hamlet of Gairsty. As he turned to battle his way up the beach against the hurricane-strength gale, he heard a massive explosion, followed by a series of huge bangs. For a few seconds the sky behind him lit up. The noise seemed to come from no more than a mile up the coast. What on earth was that?

It was 1916 - wartime - so plenty of things made no sense. When the war started there had been four brothers sharing the croft with Mum and Dad. Now there were just two and one of them, his younger brother Samuel, had just been conscripted for the British Army. Sam would be heading south to be fitted for his uniform and given some token training in trench warfare in the next few days. Archie, in contrast, had succeeded in pushing his claim that fishing, plus looking after his frail mother and disabled father, was a recognised Reserved Occupation.

Despite the conditions Archie decided to turn along the cliff-top toward Marwick Head rather than directly inland to his family croft. As he reached the higher ground, still keeping close to the cliff edge, he kept peering out to sea: what had happened?

And then he saw it, in the churning waves, not more than a mile offshore: the remains of a large vessel, stern in the air, angled ever more steeply towards the vertical.

It was eleven o'clock at night but it was June: in Orkney it would be light for another hour. He shielded his eyes against the driving rain but could see no lights burning on board and, worse still, no signs of lifeboats being launched. The whole tragedy must have happened inside a few minutes: presumably the crew hadn't had time for the usual response.

As he watched the vessel slid slowly, inexorably, beneath the waves. Then there was nothing. He could hardly believe it. If he hadn't seen it for himself there would have nothing to demonstrate that anything untoward had happened. Archie removed his cap and gave a silent prayer.

It was as he walked back towards his boat that he heard a creaking sound from down below. It must be a life boat: someone had survived the disaster. Archie hurried on down until he could see a way of clambering down the cliff, and then headed down the rocky shore. There were rocks and huge boulders, but beyond he could see just a single small rowing boat, with two or three people on board, battling against the waves.

'Ahoy,' shouted Archie, waving ferociously.

One of the rowers heard him and redoubled his efforts. But there must be some rip tide operating here that pulled them along the coast rather than in. They swept on faster than Archie could move on the barnacle- encrusted rocks. He could only follow slowly in their wake.

As he got to the next little promontory and peered over he saw the boat was in even more trouble. The lifeboat had been thrown into a reef of rocks that was running out to sea. The vessel was upside down and its occupants thrashing around in the water.

Archie waded in and struggled to reach them but for two folk he was too late. Only the third was still alive and he was comatose, nestling among the shore-line boulders.

Archie was over six foot tall, but the passenger was even taller. Even so there was no choice: he had to be dragged up the shore and away from the deadly waves. Fifteen minutes of hard toil saw him shifted to a small cave : it must have been scooped out by millions of years of waves pounding on the sandstone cliffs.

Archie checked his breathing: the survivor was still alive, though only just. He needed help and he needed it fast.

It took Archie forty minutes to fetch Samuel from his croft in Gairsty. The younger man had already gone to bed after a final glass of whisky and had to be roused from his slumbers. The pair brought a primitive stretcher with them and a lamp. Archie would have brought others too but the war had taken its toll: there was no-one else around now under the age of fifty.

'The bloke was pretty far gone already. We may be too late,' warned Archie as the pair hastened along the track down to the shore.

The gale was still blowing fiercely. Despite this he managed to light the lamp. The victim was unconscious but there were still signs of life: whatever else, this man was a survivor. As gently as they could the brothers eased him onto the stretcher, covered him with a blanket and then started the struggle back towards the croft.

It took half an hour but at long last they were out of the rain and biting wind. The peat fire was still smouldering as they dragged him into the main room and laid him beside its residual warmth. Archie was thankful that his parents were still asleep and shut their bedroom door. Then he lit the main paraffin lamp and gave the survivor his full attention.

There were cuts on his head where he'd hit rocks as he'd been washed ashore but no obvious signs of broken bones or disfigured limbs.

'We'd better get him out of these wet clothes and into something dry,' said Sam. Between them they eased off the man's trench coat and uniform, and lastly his underwear. It was all ringing wet. Finally they replaced these clothes with Archie's Sunday best.

'That's a magnificent moustache,' observed Sam as they worked. 'In fact, he looks like the bloke on the Army recruitment poster, you know, "Your country needs you".'

'The one Jamie and Donald fell for when the war started,' replied Archie. He had never really come to terms with the loss of his two brothers. Both had fallen in the trenches in the early days of the war.

He mused for a moment. 'But it can't be Kitchener: he's a key member of the War Cabinet, down in London.'

'But it might be a lookalike,' said Sam. 'You know, someone sent up to the North of Scotland to strut about, raise morale and boost recruitment.'

Right now Archie was more concerned with the man's health than his identity. 'Listen. I think he's going down. His breathing's getting shallower. We need proper medical help.'

'There's no-one around here. The nearest doctor will be in Stromness: twenty miles away. And how will we send a message? It's hardly the night for travel.'

Unsure, the brothers looked at one another for inspiration.

Then the man, sounding delirious, started to mumble. 'K . . . Khrtm.'

'Sam, that sounds like Khartoum. D'you remember? This must be Lord Horatio Herbert Kitchener of Khartoum.'

With supreme effort the man took a breath and continued. 'Huge army of natives . . . they didn't have weapons like the British Army. Their scythes . . . no match for our machine guns. War paint couldn't keep out the bullets. We mowed 'em down. Eleven thousand in a day. God save the King.'

It was the man's final words. He breathed once more and passed away.

There was silence in the croft for a few moments.

Archie swallowed hard. 'You know, the best lookalike in the world is not going to stick to his lines as he approaches death. I've not the faintest ideas what he was doing up here but I reckon that really was Kitchener.'

'Heroic to the last.'

'Heroic? He used modern weapons on primitive tribesmen. No wonder he was "successful". That's not valour, Sam, its brute force. The same mindless attitude that lost us Jamie and Donald. And will probably lose us you too.'

Sam was struggling with conflicting emotions. Kitchener was the Head of the British Army, the man everyone was taught to look up to. He'd been brought up practically to worship him. But he had respect for his older brother too; and Archie didn't seem to hold the man in that high regard.

'Maybe it's a pity you rescued him, Archie. It would have been better if he'd died at sea along with the rest of the crew.'

Archie looked at the figure lying on the floor and then across to the framed telegrams hanging on the wall. It was the death of their two elder sons, he knew, that had broken his parents. And it was this warmonger – Lord Kitchener of Khartoum - that had dragged them into harm's way.

'You know, Sam, I don't want this man to be given a hero's funeral. I don't want him to be festooned with honours as part of this bloody war. Only you and I know he died in this croft. I reckon we've one more job to do tonight and that's to take him somewhere that he'll never be found.'

Half an hour later, as Orkney's brief period of full summer darkness began, the lads set out once more with their stretcher. They had lived here all their lives and knew the series of paths required. Mercifully the storm seemed to have abated and it was no longer raining.

Up they went to Marwick Head. Archie had remembered there used to be peat digging up there. That would make it easy to bury Kitchener where he would never be found.

The first light was just breaking as they completed the task.

'He was a tough man,' said Sam. 'Sure, he was a man of his time, an Imperialist when the British Empire needed heroes. But for better or for worse we won't see his type again.'

'God rest his soul,' prayed Archie. Whatever his inner feelings it was not his place to pass judgement.

Sam went off to France a month later. He was there just in time for the Somme offensive. Three weeks later his parents received another telegram, telling them that they had lost another son killed in action.

Archie never told anyone of the events of that night. But when the local community decided that they would erect a huge tower on Marwick Head – the Kitchener Memorial - he did make a small contribution towards the costs. He also ensured that the tower was sited not far from the place where he alone knew Kitchener's body now lay.

There were too many deaths in war. Every one of them was a tragedy.

Horatio Herbert Kitchener was one of 725 men drowned when HMS Hampshire hit a mine off the west coast of the Orkneys in June 1916 and sank in minutes. He had been sailing to reassure the Russians of continued Allied support. Coming just a few days after the inconclusive battle of Jutland, his death shocked the nation.

After the war local citizens erected a fifty foot high stone tower on Marwick Head in his memory. Kitchener's body was never found.

10. COMPETING LOYALTIES

A sudden knock and then a dishevelled Ted Cooke-Yarborough rushed in. As usual he was running late.

'Sorry I'm late, Sir John. My experimental automatic lawn mower wouldn't switch off. I didn't mind it destroying the flowerbed but then it got loose in the road.'

Sir John Cockroft, calm, smartly suited, Nobel Prize Winner for physics in 1933, now Head of the Atomic Energy Research Establishment at Harwell, looked at him with some disdain. 'Is that why there's grease on your sleeve, Ted – or was that some earlier "experiment"?'

Ted glanced down, saw the problem, looked mildly embarrassed. Smart appearance was not high on his ambitions. 'Trouble is, Sir John, there's so many things I want to do – and only twenty four hours in the day. We've so much to catch up after the war. That's why I'm after the Board's approval and funding to start work on a new "computer"'.

'So that's what you call it – a computer. Yes, I've got your proposal here. Dr Fuchs and I were trying to make head or tail of it.'

The third person in the office, Harwell's Head of Physics, Klaus Fuchs, was sitting awkwardly at the end of the executive desk, looking less than enthusiastic. He took off his glasses to give them a polish then turned to the flamboyant Section Head.

'It's a matter of priorities, Ted. You estimate that this new gadget will cost tens of thousands of pounds. That's a lot of money for this Establishment. It means someone else will lose out and other research won't get done. How will that help us develop the theory of atomic energy?'

He hadn't been invited to do so but Ted decided to sit down. He'd got off to a bad start: it would be best to begin again.

What was going on? There were lots of wet blankets in the Harwell set-up but he'd been hoping these two would be his best supporters. Ted was incorrigibly optimistic about all his ideas but this proposal was a special favourite. He knew the key person to convince was Sir John Cockroft.

'We all know Harwell has been set up as the UK's premier research establishment, Sir John. To turn academic knowledge into applications for the modern world. It's not much talked about, yet, but the concept of a "computer" – an advanced calculator that uses electronic circuits to think for itself – was arguably one of the big intellectual advances of the war. Britain has some of the best brains in this field. Right now Harwell is one of the few places in the UK where those academic riches could be turned into something practical.'

Cockcroft glanced up at the photograph on the wall, showing him receiving his award from the Nobel Prize Committee. 'I didn't need one of these "computer" things to split the atom, Ted. Just top quality collaborative brain power. Tell me again why we need the thing. Persuade me it's not another of your wayward experiments.'

This was much harder work than he'd imagined. Ted had been

looking forward to a lively three-way technical discussion of the design.

'The outline I've presented, Sir John, is for a machine that will do repeat calculations rapidly and reliably. At the simplest level, right now, it would reduce the number of typists and clerks working in the Admin block – paying wages, tracking expenses and so on. There are hundreds of 'em. So either those people could be used somewhere else in Harwell or they could be replaced, over time, by top-class scientists. I admit it's expensive, but I estimate the machine would recover its development costs in four years.'

Dr Fuchs intervened. 'Ah. So your main justification is to achieve greater operating efficiency?'

'At one level. But there's also a much bigger argument about scientific progress. One day, I believe, computers will be able to do things which are far more complicated than routine administration.'

He laughed, 'One day, long after we've gone, they might help land a man on the moon. But we'll only unpack their potential if we start down the trail. It's a road where the UK can – and I believe must - be in the lead.'

'Ha. The British and their imperial tendency – always it is the thing which drives you on.'

Cooke-Yarborough remembered that Dr Fuchs had been born in Germany. No doubt that would give him a different perspective on UK research. It crossed his mind, why was a German so high up in a UK research establishment? But it was not his place to question credentials.

'In the post-war world, Dr Fuchs, we are seeking collaboration wherever possible. The United Nations, for example. The new European Common Market. We must all avoid the mistakes of the past. Try not to amplify international tension.'

'But, Klaus, to be at the forefront of computer development – that sounds a prize worth scooping.' Sir John had ambitions for his establishment as well as his country. Maybe this proposal was not as bizarre as he'd first thought. 'How far have you got with collaboration, anyway?'

'There are developments in Manchester with Alan Turing. But there's also a machine being built in Cambridge – "EDSAC" is what they call it. I've been over there several times to see it in progress.'

'Is this not just a device to help you win the next war?' Dr Fuchs looked far from convinced.

'I do not know what you were doing in the war, Dr Fuchs. My own biggest contribution was a device installed in our bombers. It picked up radio signals, identified the strongest frequency and allowed that to be jammed so enemy radar no longer worked – kept our bombers a little safer.'

'Gentlemen, gentlemen, now is not the time to be replaying the war. Ted, Dr Fuchs is a naturalised Briton – been here since 1933. He played a very important role in theoretical physics, both here and in the United States.'

That sounded alright, though Ted was not completely convinced. One of his contacts in Cambridge had hinted, after they'd downed their third pints, that there was something suspicious about the man.

'But leaving aside the war, Sir John, will there be funds available for this project?'

This was the crucial question which the meeting had to answer. There was a pause. Sir John looked across at Dr Fuchs.

But before either could speak the phone rang.

After work Ted took his deputy out for a drink. He'd not said anything in the office but they knew an inn in the nearby village of Blewbury where they could talk in private and off the record. Ted ordered two pints of Directors and the pair moved to the most remote alcove.

'So what happened, Ted? Do we have approval?'

'I think so, Dick. It was all very odd.'

'In what way?'

'I was just getting into my pitch when the phone rang. Sir John Cockcroft picked it up and listened for a long time. He looked very upset. Then he said something like "So it's all over". But he wasn't talking to me, he was addressing Dr Fuchs.'

'Oh, our mystery physicist was there as well, was he?'

'He was. After that Sir John put down the phone, turned to me and said, 'OK, it's approved. But you'd better go now." He'd said the key words and I didn't hang about.'

'But you said it was "odd"? What exactly was odd about him giving approval. After all, it's a brilliant concept.'

'He said it in the tone he might have used in approving a special week's leave. As though it didn't really matter. Whereas you and I know that if we can make this work computers could be the tool of the future.'

'Sounds as if his mind was elsewhere.'

'Probably. As I walked down the corridor I met two policemen heading towards me. Then, when I was outside, I saw one of those police vans – a Black Maria, I think they call 'em – was waiting outside.'

'Not just odd, I'd call that downright peculiar. No wonder he was distracted. Was that all?'

'Well, you can imagine, I was very curious. So I glanced back once or twice. And when I looked the last time, I saw Dr Klaus Fuchs being bundled into the back of the Maria and then driven away. So we may never see him here again.'

'You know, I always thought he was too clever by half.'

'Look on the bright side, Dick. It may not be what he'd intended, but at least we've got approval to develop one of the world's first computers.'

It was three months later that Dr Klaus Fuchs, once Head of Physics at Harwell, was sentenced at the Old Bailey to fourteen years in prison. He had confessed to systematically spying for Russia.

The outline of this meeting – which really happened, though all three attendees are now dead - is recorded in the National Computing Museum at Bletchley.

11. WEDDING WOBBLES

I'd had a rough life before I met Jeremy. After a bad start I'd fallen for drugs and, if it hadn't been for that Yeldall Manor rehab programme near Wargrave, I'd have sunk without trace.

Jeremy was a wise and wealthy man whose weekend hobby was providing vintage cars for couples at weddings. He was also a long-term supporter of Yeldall. Last year he came to a Manor Open Evening, met one or two of us who had progressed as far as Day Release and learned that I too had a love for old cars.

Two days later I received a residential job offer: to keep his pair of cars maintained and polished; and to be the second driver on days when he had double bookings.

The pay was modest but it was a second chance and I grabbed it with both hands. I'd be living out in the country, in the stables behind Jeremy's country house, but that was no problem at all: it was a real opportunity to chuck drugs for good. It gave me chance to drive Jeremy's classic Austin and his 1928 Bentley, both rich shades of maroon, round his estate. Later, when I was more confident, I was allowed to drive one or other – usually the Austin - to the occasional wedding.

By the time I'd been there six months I was a proficient driver and a new man. The world of drugs was a long way behind me.

The bookings behind this story came in at much the same time. I'd progressed by now to administering the car hire, so took an interest in the arrangements. What was unusual was that both weddings were on the same day and at adjacent churches, St Andrew the Great and St Andrew the Martyr, both in the tangle of streets off Reading's Oxford Road.

'STAG and STAM, Albert,' said Jeremy, when I told him. 'Poles apart theologically. Both designed by the same architect around 1900, though, so they look almost identical. Cynics suggest he economised by giving both lots the same design: relied on neither noticing until it was too late. Well, well. I see the dates and times clash so you'll have to drive for one of them.'

It was agreed I would take Alexandra and James from STAG in the Austin while Jeremy took Alice and Jim away from STAM in the Bentley.

'That gives you the young couple, Albert. I'll handle the older pair, we can all be sedate together. STAG generally has the bigger congregation, so it should be a cheerful occasion – maybe even rowdy. I'm sure you won't let them down.'

I was extra diligent at fitting glistening white ribbons onto the bonnets of both cars.

One snag I had missed beforehand – maybe because I was living out in the country - was the activities of British Gas as they replaced gas pipes in the centre of Reading. You might have thought that this firm would foresee the disruption and would stagger the work: it really didn't all need to be done at once.

Of course, you would have been wrong. When British Gas installs new pipes it does so on a grand scale: it wants everyone to know how seriously it takes new infrastructure. So when I turned off Oxford Road I found myself in a maze of temporary one-way streets, every one with road works and some with traffic lights.

It being Saturday, though, there was no-one at work laying new gas pipes.

But the area was far from quiet. There were other workers on the scene: a platoon of traffic wardens, eager to fine those car drivers who had fallen into one or other trap. For the random pattern of road works meant that some streets were inaccessible from all directions, whereas others could be entered but not left. Since all the roads had yellow lines and restricted parking, it was almost impossible to avoid breaking one regulation or another in moving round the area.

The trick was not being caught while doing so.

Jeremy had the easier task. Alice lived almost opposite STAM so did not need a car to take her to the church service. His work would only begin when the wedding was over.

I had a more conventional sequence. I collected Alex and her father and was glad to have the older man's advice on finding the church. They were regular worshippers at STAG, I gathered, so had figured out a way through the gas works maze.

That was fine until the pair were delivered. The next phase was supposed to be that I reversed into the car park and waited until the service was over.

That would have been okay except that British Gas engineers had blocked off the entrance to the church car park for some no-doubt essential piece of engineering. I had no choice but to keep driving slowly round the area until the service was over.

A small-scale street map of Reading sat on the seat beside me. But there was no SatNav on a car this old and my map did not show the latest configuration of viable streets. It was a matter of trial and error. I was also conscious of Jeremy's pride in his cars and the need to avoid scratching the Austin.

All in all a traumatic experience.

And then, it seemed a miracle, I was inching down a street when I saw a church door open and a bride and groom emerge.

I did not hesitate. I pulled in alongside them, jumped out and rushed to open the back door. The couple seemed slightly surprised but took my lead and sat themselves inside. Then I rushed back to the driver's seat and restarted the engine before a traffic warden could catch me.

Though, I thought, even the most stone-hearted warden would find it hard to give a ticket to the driver of a bridal car as he was picking up the happy couple.

For a few moments there was silence. It took all my energy to find a way out of the maze and the couple were in a dream world of their own.

Five minutes later I reached the Oxford Road and breathed a sigh of relief. I still couldn't go at any speed but at least I knew where I was.

For the first time I glanced in my mirror at the couple behind. Crumbs, the woman had aged a lot during the service. Going in she had been a carefree twenty-something; now she looked to be well into her thirties, with all the cares of the world on her shoulders.

What could possibly have been said in the address that aged her so abruptly? I shuffled sideways so the mirror showed me the groom. I hadn't seen him before the service, of course, but the man was well into his forties. To my mind that made him practically a cradle-snatcher. Never mind a reception, ought I not to be

79

heading for the nearest police station? I could still remember where that was from my other life.

What had happened? Maybe the vicar had dwelt too long on the bridal obligation "in sickness and in health" and the girl had taken it too much to heart?

Reaching the familiarity of Oxford Road seemed to release the pair from their private rapture.

'I hadn't expected we'd go off quite so quickly,' observed the man. 'Weren't there supposed to be photographs at the church?'

'Yes, the car was remarkably punctual,' the bride replied. 'It'll be a much more photogenic venue, anyway, at Ufton Court. Mind you, the guests will take some time to get there.'

'It doesn't matter, my dear, we can enjoy time on our own till they reach us.' He gave his new wife a gentle squeeze.

Ufton Court, eh? I could have sworn the application said the reception was at Maple Durham. I knew where the place was, anyway. This seemed an unusual wedding: best to get there without asking too many questions.

Back at St Andrew the Martyr, I learned later, there was a certain amount of panic. Bride and groom had walked serenely out the West End door at the end of the service and completely disappeared. The photographer was particularly baffled. He had a long list of groups to be coordinated into place outside the side of the church, but he could hardly start that without the happy couple.

The best man and chief bridesmaid, Simon and Mary, had only met once before the service but quickly joined forces. A rapid search was conducted. Their friends surely could not have gone far. Was there a crypt they had slipped down into? Or a special place, with trees in their autumn colours, somewhere in the churchyard?

The congregation was asked to wait inside the church as the search widened to the surrounding streets. Three streets along, they spotted a possible clue: a gleaming Bentley, white ribbons attached, parked in the loading bay beside a small supermarket.

'D'you reckon that's the car booked for Alice and Jim?' asked Simon.

'Let's ask him,' replied Mary. In her stress she tapped rather too hard on the window and the driver, Jeremy, who had been having a few minutes snooze, jumped several inches into the air.

In general he had learned to ignore such interruptions but the two who had accosted him were very smartly dressed in wedding-like attire. Slowly, making sure he was fully awake, he wound down the window.

'Are you the driver for the wedding of Alice and Jim?' asked Simon.

'I am,' Jeremy replied, 'Ready to take you to Ufton Court. But was I not supposed to pick you up at the church?'

'There was a mix-up,' Simon replied. 'The service finished sooner than expected. Can you take us from here, please?'

He noticed Mary was looking at him questioningly but he ignored her. The driver had no doubt; he leapt out and opened the door for the pair. A moment later, a second vintage car was threading its way through the Reading streets and out towards Ufton Court.

The Austin was the first to arrive at the reception. The trees in the approach drive were shedding their leaves, a gardener was busy scooping them into a wheelbarrow. I drove up the drive, pulled in to the Tudor mansion and discharged my passengers.

I gave a sigh of relief: I assumed my task for the day was completed. Sometimes I fear for my grip on sanity.

I was heading for the exit when I was surprised to meet a second vintage car coming in, a Bentley, also covered with white ribbons. It was Jeremy. Something was badly wrong.

I pulled over onto one grass verge and the Bentley did the same on the other.

'The Winning Hand?' I suggested, naming the pub where I'd turned off from the A4.

Jeremy nodded and then drove on. There was a need to discuss which of us had brought the real bride and groom here, and who had the imposters.

And if our two wedding cars were attending this reception, what on earth was happening at the other?

I saw Jeremy discharge his passengers at Ufton Court and then turn to follow me to the *rendez vous*.

In my mirror I saw the couple I'd brought delightedly welcoming the pair from the second car. I was no longer sure who any of them were but at least they knew each other. It would stop Ufton Court feeling too empty.

At St Andrew's the Great, I would learn later, the cake reception continued. No car was on hand to take this bride and groom off to their reception at Maple Durham.

But for the time being it did not matter. There were acres of cake; and most guests did not care where they were mingling as long as there was plenty of champagne. The mood of the gathering moved from happy-clappy to burpy-chirpy.

That Saturday the police were undertaking checks on the A4, a road famed for speeding and other dubious activity. Two policemen, taking a break, followed me into the Winning Hand and one recognised me from my former life.

'What are you doing here?' These days, I explained, I was a chauffeur. I'd just dropped a bridal couple off at Ufton Court.

It was unfortunate Jeremy joined us a few moments later with an identical story.

'Ah, a double wedding?' asked the policeman, smiling.

'Not exactly,' I replied.

'So why two wedding cars?' I could see doubts emerging. 'Could you give us the names of the happy couples, sir?'

This was getting tricky. I was about to hazard a guess when my phone rang. 'Hello, is that Albert, the wedding car chauffeur?'

'It is.'

'Great. This is the best man, calling from St Andrews the Great. Where on earth are you?'

'I got caught up in the gas works, had to move on. Actually, I'm just talking to the police.'

'Stuff the police, you're needed here. As soon as possible, if not sooner. We're almost out of champagne.'

Looking back, it was a mercy we hadn't had a drink. A pity, though, that we were accosted before we had had chance to find out how our stories fitted together.

Mercifully the police let us go and the Austin was free to reappear at the STAG entrance. This time Jeremy had elected to sit beside me, acting as my navigator.

'You guys have such an easy life,' commented Alex's dad, as the happy couple climbed on board and I prepared to drive the Austin to its second reception of the day.

I mused that, after Jeremy and I had got the couple to Maple Durham, I would need to drive him all the way back to the Winning Hand on the other side of Reading to pick up the Bentley. Once again there would be two ribbon-festooned wedding cars parked outside.

I could only hope we would not be accosted again. It was getting steadily harder to disentangle the role of each car and each driver in each wedding.

Jeremy spotted my silence and realised we needed to respond. He turned to the father of the bride. 'You'd be surprised, sir; it has its moments.'

But it would be best not to try and explain. Some wedding detail is better left lost in the confetti.

12. DOUBLE JEOPARDY

I heard the rumour as I walked down the road. They were going to reopen the lowest level of Levant Tin Mine.

It was 1929. For ten years the lowest part of the mine, which ran out under the sea, had been closed off. Not long after the end of the Great War the main shaft had collapsed without warning and many had died, including some of my best colleagues. I had only escaped by toiling for an hour up a long-forgotten stairway.

The mine had limped on, production well down, which was just as well as worldwide demand for tin had dropped too. But now, it seemed, there was a chance of fresh sales. New management had arrived and a combined operation was coming into place, partnering Geever Mine next door.

And in this new spirit of joint enterprise someone had recalled the higher productivity of the tunnels that ran out under the sea.

I could have told them that. But I'd have made sure they also heard the other side of the argument. The working shifts were shorter: men had to walk out under the sea for hundreds of yard before they could start digging for the ore. And pumps had to run continually, day and night, to keep the flooding in check.

For though the tunnels were intended to run twenty or thirty feet beneath the ocean floor, that floor was far from level. In one or two places you could hear the sea pounding above you and seawater trickling down. For all sorts of reasons I'd been glad when those tin-ore mining faces had been closed.

85

The rumour was confirmed at a mine workers' meeting later that week. Much better pumps available these days, they said. Credit, no doubt, to the war. Draining trenches at the Front must have been a priority for both sides. They also announced there would be special rates of pay for all those opting to work under the sea.

'Are you tempted, Fred?' asked one of my colleagues, as we left the meeting.

'Huh, the pay would need to be very special indeed,' I replied.

I was in a routine now and had no wish to change. My wife Hilda had got herself a job teaching in St Just Primary School. We were still poor, by the standards of the rest of the country, but we had our croft and we were solvent.

It turned out, though, when the details were announced later, that a more honest way of putting it was that all existing rates would drop by 25%, while the "special rates" for working under the sea would stay the same. It wasn't much of a incentive scheme.

To my surprise, management pressed me to go down into the depths again.

'You've got the experience, see, Fred. The youngsters will take heed of you.'

I was dubious but in the end we struck a deal. I would do the under-sea work for six months and train up new foremen. Then go back to working on reduced pay but at the higher level.

Three months later the work to clear the lower levels began.

The new pumps were installed and started draining the sea water that had accumulated in the old workings. I was glad to see they were efficient and reliable: the water level started to drop and kept falling. Gradually the debris that had accumulated over the years was brought to the shaft and hauled back to the surface.

The piles of mine waste surrounding the Levant area grew ever larger.

Finally came the day when the first shift of miners was despatched in search of ore. I was among them.

I had one additional fear, as well as the natural fears of working hundreds of feet down and out under the sea. For the last time I had been there, I had been attacked by Harry, a huge miner who was at the time married to Hilda. He had accused me – falsely - of trying to steal his wife and had tried to kill me. But by some miracle he had caught his own head and died instead.

Were his remains still there, I wondered, and would I have questions to answer?

In the aftermath of the 1919 mining disaster the shift details on that day had been lost or destroyed. That had emerged when I'd tried to check on the positions of one or two missing colleagues.

I'd never said a word to anyone about what happened. So even if Harry's body was found (how long did bodies take to reduce to skeletons?) and was recognised in a remote tunnel, and even if suspicion was raised on exactly how he had died, no-one would know, in 1929, that I had been the one alongside him ten years earlier.

My conscience was clear but I could see it didn't look good. I hoped I would never be cross-examined.

For a long time I thought I'd got away with it. It took some time but Harry's bones were eventually scooped up with the debris in a far-off tunnel. His identity tag was still round his neck, faded and dirty, but allowing him to be identified. But there was no longer any flesh present on the body.

So you couldn't tell, now, that he had died from a wound to the head.

I was almost at the end of the six months I'd agreed to work at depth when a new manager, Thomas Cassidy, joined the company. He was a similar age to me and had worked for many years in Cambourne. They liked to think they were more progressive up there; he'd been recruited to bring some of the new ideas to Levant.

Obviously he had to start his time in West Cornwall by seeing as much of the existing mine as possible. Eventually that brought him to our workings under the sea.

I was senior foreman. I met him at the top and brought him down the oscillating ladders to the foot of the shaft myself. I was pleased to see he approved of the new water pumps installed at the bottom.

'Good design,' he commented. 'We've got that sort at Cambourne. Can't afford to risk flooding in a modern mine – especially one working under the sea.'

'But no lighting on the main tunnels?' he asked as we stumbled on. 'I bet it looked much like this last century.'

'The management always try to minimise expenditure,' I explained. 'They tell us keeping costs down is the only way we'll survive.'

'Whereas in Cambourne we say investment is the only way we'll succeed,' he replied. 'I can see we'll need some discussion on this.'

We walked on: Thomas wanted to see how far the tunnels stretched.

'Must have been somewhere around here my brother died,' he commented.

'I'm afraid a lot have died here over the years,' I replied. 'What was his name?'

'Harry.'

I tried to take his answer in my stride but I was worried. I tried to remember "my" Harry's surname but it had gone. It was ten years since I'd used it or even thought about it. Still, Harry was a common enough name.

He didn't mention it again as I showed him the new under-sea workings.

That evening, when I got home, I checked with my wife, Hilda. After all, she'd once been married to Harry, had taken his name as her own.

'He was Harry Cassidy,' she replied. 'What makes you ask?'

'Cassidy,' I repeated. 'Yes, that's right. It's his brother that's joined our management team.' I told her about Thomas's aside during our tour of the under-sea tunnels.

'Now you remind me, I seem to remember Harry had a younger brother called Thomas. The two weren't much alike, mind. Thomas was as bright as his brother was brutal. Does it bother you?'

'I'll be alright as long as he doesn't connect me with Harry,' I said. 'No reason why he should: the poor devil's been dead a long time.'

For a while Thomas had no idea I had any link with his brother. He never would, except that he started reviewing the Levant Management's paperwork – such as it was. In the course of that he came across the discovery of his brother's remains on the edge of the undersea workings.

In their sloppy way the management had regarded one more body as more of a nuisance than anything else. Much of the local churchyard was taken with victims of the mine disaster ten years earlier, including names of those lost who had never been found. The recently discovered remains of Harry had been given a quiet funeral beside them, with Thomas and the rest of the Cassidy family not even being notified.

Because it was his own brother, Thomas took it all far more seriously. How come, he asked, that Harry had died so far from the shaft; and who was working alongside him?

I could see the way the tide was running. I knew Thomas was a persistent man. After talking it over with Hilda we decided that full confession was better than drip by drip exposure.

Next day I happened to ran into Thomas on my way back from my shift.

'Thomas, would you like to come for supper with my wife and I? We may have a family connection.'

He looked surprised but pleased to be invited. His forensic methods had not made him many friends at Levant. I said I'd come to his office on the date we'd agreed and guide him to our croft.

I introduced him to Hilda as soon as he stepped inside the door. 'Thomas, this is my dear wife Hilda. And Hilda, this is Thomas

Cassidy, the brother of your previous husband.'

Thomas looked shocked. I could see his brain whirring and trying to fit pieces together.

'Let's all sit down,' I suggested. 'Then perhaps I should begin by telling you what I know about Harry.'

As calmly as I could I told them both the whole story of that dreadful night. How Harry had tried to kill me, but instead felled himself when his anvil bounced back off a low piece of roof. How I'd backed away rather than offer help. And how the mine disaster, which by pure chance happened on the same day, had eliminated all attention on the affair.

To his credit, Thomas listened like a juryman until I had finished. Then he asked me, chillingly. 'So now you're trying another way of hiding the truth?'

'Are you saying I killed him?' I shouted. 'Harry was huge, I'd never have stood a chance.'

Now Thomas was angry too. 'What I'm saying is, how odd that it all coincided with the mine disaster. Which makes me wonder, which came first?'

It took me a second to follow his meaning. 'I knew nothing about trouble in the shaft when Harry confronted me. I swear.'

'No, but he might have heard some sort of racket – and reckoned that made it a good time to settle your affairs.'

There was silence for a moment and then he turned to my wife. 'Exactly when did you and Fred start going out? Was it after Harry died – or before?'

We'd agreed Hilda would also be totally honest.

'Fred and I used to talk on our way back from the weekly choir in St Just. But we were only friends. Harry had it wrong. Nothing would ever have happened if he hadn't died.'

Thomas was silent and then gave his verdict. 'It's all too neat. You're asking me to come a long way on so little evidence. In all honesty I ought to be taking my fears to the police.'

Hilda had half expected this response. But she had one card left to play.

'Thomas, let me tell you one more thing about Harry. He was a sadistic bully. I've never told anyone but he used to beat me regularly. On Saturday nights he'd totter home from the pub and thrash me black and blue. Sometimes I was so bruised I wouldn't make church next day.'

She paused, her eyes filling with tears, and then turned towards him. 'Go to the police if you want, Thomas. But if it all comes to court, I warn you: I won't hold anything back on your brother and what he was really like.'

Thomas, turning towards her, looked dismayed. He bowed his head and covered his face in his hands. I sensed there were tears in his eyes too. Then he looked up.

'You know, Hilda, I completely believe you. Now I think about it, Harry was a bully at school. He was always in trouble; or making trouble for his fellow students. I saw his violence once or twice for myself, as did my poor mother. At least once he attacked her. You poor woman. As his wife, tucked away out of sight at home, you'd have no protection at all.'

Calmer now, he turned to me. 'Fred, I'm sorry I doubted. Let me say, I fully accept your account of what happened. It would be just like Harry to try and finish you off. It was a miracle you survived. The whole thing is so providential that it has to be true.'

13. MORE CORPSES THAN COFFINS

My first long vacation saw me back home on the Isle of Purbeck. I'd plenty of plans all right but most of them needed money. So before I could go off with my university friends to explore the wider world I had to find a summer job. Which was why, after a couple of abortive weeks searching for jobs that would make some use of my mathematics, I ended up at the local Crematorium.

There were plenty of sniggers from former school friends but we were no longer that close anyway. This was a regular job with a living wage and predictable hours. I didn't even have to work weekends. Every set of funeral mourners was different and my tasks ranged from arranging flowers and hoovering the hall (every morning) and cleaning out the furnace (every Friday) to taking readings on gas use. I also acted as an usher at services when no-one else was taking the rôle.

In some small way I felt I was being a useful member of society.

There had been a change of staff at the Crem just before I arrived. An old man who'd been there for years had left suddenly. He'd been replaced by a well-built, bearded man under the age of thirty who was something of a hunk. I gathered Gerald commuted from Swanage every day on the local steam train. I just had to get there from Corfe village on my push bike. A year of cycling in Cambridge had left me fairly fit.

It wasn't long before Gerald and I became friends. We were the only full-time staff there. It started slowly and I tried to keep it low key. Having "a funeral man as a boyfriend" sounded even worse (even to my ears) than "working full-time at the Crem".

It was in my third week that I noticed that someone was attending the services rather often. It wasn't easy to spot. The man had a variety of coats, hats and gloves for different appearances. Sometime he wore spectacles or shades, other times he didn't. Once he even came with a walking stick. But he usually sat in the corner at the back; and disappeared, once the service was over, extremely quickly.

After a while I decided to play a game of my own. When I saw him at the back I would slip out at the start of the last hymn and hide myself in the trees beside the main cemetery exit gate, ready to see him leave.

The puzzle was that as far as I could see he didn't leave at all – at least not in a car he was driving. Some funeral cars had dark windows and I couldn't tell who was in the rear seats. But I couldn't play my game very often or I too might become the focus of special attention. I didn't want that.

I wasn't sure whether to bother Gerald with my worries. He had plenty of responsibility, making sure the Crem ran smoothly for a succession of undertakers. By comparison one unknown mourner was no problem. And when we went out together on our first date, a meal in Corfe, I didn't want to prattle on about work-related topics. Nor did I mention that I was a maths student at Cambridge. I sensed Gerald's formal education had finished much earlier.

Even so, it bothered me. If all was above board then I could see no reason for the man to keep changing his appearance. He might enjoy funerals, say, or even be doing a PhD on the types of hymns used. But if there was something underhand going on, what on earth could it be? Surely no-one could be acquainted with that many dead people over such a short period in a small area like Purbeck?

And if an exchange was taking place with another mourner – documents, say, or even drugs - why on earth do it in a crematorium rather than a local pub?

It was true we didn't have CCTV cameras inside the Crem but there were plenty of other places without cameras that would be equally convenient.

It occurred to me, though, that if there was something outside the law I had better be very careful in my investigations.

My next observation was that Mr Black (as I had decided to call him) was never there on Tuesdays or Thursdays. And the numbers of funerals on those days was much lower. So could anything be said about the funerals on the other days that did not hold on Tuesdays or Thursdays?

I had little to do most evenings and it was easy to take the Crematorium log book home with me. The raw data did not take long to unravel. Three undertakers appeared only on the start, middle or end days of each week; they never came on Tuesdays or Thursdays. In my mind I termed the three "Messrs Red, Yellow and Green".

That struck me as very odd. An undertaker would have little say in when their funerals took place. It would depend on all sorts of factors, for example the dates suitable for mourners. It was conceivable that a funeral director could keep one day a week free as their day of rest. But for three undertakers each to keep the same two days was inconceivable.

It only made any sense if they were all linked in some way with Mr Black.

Now I had slightly more idea of the pattern I notice other oddities about the services involved the "Black undertakers". There were repeat mourners at their funerals. Again it was not obvious. The women would change coats and hats between appearances and might partner different men at different services. But it wasn't entirely the same cast at each. There were plenty of single-service mourners among the repeats.

Thinking about it, I wondered if the multi-mourners came along for appearances sake, lest no one else turned up.

And that made me wonder if the "Black funerals" were real send-offs at all.

It was fortunate that my daily work was by now routine, so it did not stop me thinking. As I continued to ponder, it occurred to me that a Crematorium with dishonest management would be in a position to offer a very distinct service to the criminal community. For this was the one place in the whole of society where dead bodies could be reduced to ash without any questions being asked. Of course some paperwork would be needed; but with a small circle of corrupt undertakers that would be easy.

And if one had to choose a Crematorium to make this unique offering, then surely it would be better in the back of beyond where high-level supervision was light, rather than, say, the inner city. One with very few permanent staff. And you'd want it to be as far away as possible from where the criminal deaths had occurred in the first place.

As I reached these conclusions I started to worry. This was not just a few oddities, there could be major criminals behind them. It was a relief to relax on Tuesdays and Thursdays: I needed to be on my guard on the other days.

Should I go to the police? But all I had at the moment were suspicions, with no hard evidence to back them up. I was the shortest student in my year. I could imagine an avuncular policeman ruffling my curly hair and telling me 'it would be best to leave all this to the grown ups'.

I continued to do my job and to keep watch. Then I noticed something else about services dealing with Messrs Red, Yellow or Green. In some cases the coffin seemed to be extremely heavy. There were more pall bearers than usual and they tottered down the aisle, sometimes putting the coffin down with a bump.

Whereas at other times the coffin seemed oddly light. I was watching carefully now and sensed that these pall bearers were only pretending to take a heavy weight.

And none of these variations happened on Tuesday or Thursday.

The only way for it to make sense, I decided, was that in some cremations two bodies were being turned to ash at the same time; whereas in others no body was being cremated at all.

It took a while for it to make sense. I could guess why it might be useful to dispose of a second body – say of someone who was supposed to have disappeared or gone abroad. But why go through all the rigmarole of a funeral service if no-one had died?

Maybe, though, the person had died earlier and for some reason the claimed date of death and burial needed to be delayed?

Or perhaps they had been done away in some dark cellar and been buried at sea, then a relative had innocently asked to attend the funeral?

Then it occurred to me that I had data to support or refute my ideas. I had been told to keep track of gas usage. Being a mathematician I had not just done this every week but jotted down the meter reading after every funeral. I had wondered if there might be some connection between gas use and air temperature. That evening I transferred my readings to a spreadsheet and worked out the gas use at each service over the five weeks I had now been employed.

Then, as I looked at the readings by day of week, the pattern was clear. On Tuesdays and Thursdays the gas use was practically the same at every service. Whereas on the other days there was a significant number when usage was almost fifty percent higher and others where it was fifty percent lower. It was only in the last week that I had written down which services Mr Black attended; but I saw that on every one of these the usage was either too high or too low.

It was evidence of a sort. To add to this I decided to check the whereabouts of Messrs Red, Yellow and Green. There were addresses for all the undertakers in the Crematorium log book but now I looked at these ones properly they seemed artificial. All three were in Wareham and I decided to check them out.

My parents normally did their weekly shop in Wareham. I cadged a lift next time they went and wandered round the town as they shopped. Soon I realised that all three undertaker addresses did not exist. The streets were there but there were no signs of any undertakers' premises.

So what was Gerald's role in all this? I had been careful to give nothing away in our weekly meals in Corfe. I had seen nothing to link him directly with Mr Black. He might be entirely innocent. I wondered, though, if any pressure had been put on his older predecessor to stand aside.

As time went on it was getting harder to keep my ideas to myself. Gerald, too, seemed to be asking more questions of me. I had been discreet but perhaps not discreet enough?

'So how long d'you plan to work at the Crem?' he asked, as we waited for our order at the Red Lion.

'Just the summer,' I replied. 'My parents insisted I did something to earn my keep. How about you?'

'My uncle got me the job,' he replied. 'I'll stick it for a while. It could be a lot worse.' He sighed. 'I'm glad you and I don't have to dig graves.'

I wondered if his uncle was Mr Black but couldn't think of any way of framing the question. If had had any link at all then the less he knew of my ideas the better. Fortunately our haddock, scampi and chips arrived at that point and disrupted our conversation.

The next morning was Friday, the day I had to be in at seven to clean out the furnace, long before the services began. This was the worst part of my job. The furnace had some residual heat from the day before but if I left it till the evening I would be scorched.

You might be wondering why the furnace needed cleaning. Surely all the ash should be scooped up and handed over to the mourners? Well yes, most of it was. There was a tray holding the coffins as they slid into the furnace; most ash would be left there and handed over. But there was a residue in the bottom that needed cleaning out once a week and it was my job to do so. There was not much space: it was a good job I was very small.

There was no-one else about. The first time I'd done this I'd emerged covered in sweat with my funeral-attending clothes covered in dust. After that I'd brought old clothes but even so I emerged caked in sweat. This morning it was hot with no-one else here. Quickly I stepped out of my jeans and tee shirt and unfastened the small side door into the furnace. It was still warm inside. I left the door open to disperse heat and give me some light as I started work. I opened a cover in the far corner, ready to remove the dust I would sweep towards it.

Then I heard voices.

One was Gerald's. The other I didn't recognise but from what I'd learned the night before it might well be Mr Black. Then I heard Gerald address him as "uncle".

I stopped work, partly to avoid being found here and partly to hear as much as I could.

Gerald was speaking. 'The thing is, uncle, I've told Miss Goode nothing at all. But she's bright. Last night I learned she's studying at Cambridge. I'm sure she's on to you; I've watched her eyeing you all this last week. And your frequent change of clothes hasn't helped at all.'

'We must keep it quiet. I doubt she's told anyone else or we'd have the authorities round. And look, we've got the mechanism right here that can remove her completely.'

I heard him bang on the wall of the furnace. 'Ouch, it's still warm.'

'Uncle, look. Those are her clothes. She must be stripped for action, already inside.'

'A girl that knows her place, eh. Ideal. Well, shut the door quickly. How d'you turn this thing on?'

The furnace door banged shut and I heard the outside bolt slide shut. I was left quivering inside in pitch darkness.

Suddenly I remembered the cover in the corner. It wasn't very wide but I was slim; the alternative was a hideously painful death as I was fried alive.

I found the corner and knelt down: my hands felt its edge. Swiftly I lowered my legs and lower body down the hole and then, seizing the edge, I let my upper body fall. Desperate for a way of protecting myself from the heat to come, I pulled the cover close over me.

Just as I did so I heard gas jetting into the furnace and then a whoosh as it ignited.

The roar of the fiery furnace provided some cover against the noise of me sliding down the shaft. Then I found myself in a storage cellar beneath the Crem.

I remained motionless as I sat down and regained my breath. I could hardly believe it: someone had made a deliberate attempt on my life. But I knew my only chance of staying alive was if they believed they had been successful.

I'd never been in the cellar before but there was a trickle of light from a dirty window, inside a railing at one end. Gradually my eyes adjusted and I oriented myself.

I decided that I daren't try to leave the Crem until the funerals for the day were over and Mr Black and Gerald were off the site. I was still dressed only in my underwear but fortunately the furnace burning above kept the cellar warm. I did not dare move far in case I knocked something over that would be heard by mourners in the chapel above.

I grew increasingly hungry and thirsty over the day but that was a small price to pay for being alive.

From time to time I could hear the sad music from the chapel above. The piano played but there was little noise from anyone singing. Then, after many hours, the last service ended.

Even then I wasn't certain Black and Gerald had left. I waited until daylight was fading in the far window. I could hear nothing at all above me. I couldn't stay here forever; where was the way out?

Slowly, carefully, I explored the cellar. Until, to my joy, I found a staircase that I judged must emerge near the organ. I crept up: there was a door at the top but was it locked? By some miracle it was not. The door opened towards me and I saw a clutter of pew cushions that had been stacked on the other side.

I could hear no noise and could see no lights. Maybe, at long last, I was on the road to safety?

Carefully I made my way towards the women's cloakroom. My funeral-attending clothes were still on their peg and I slipped them on. At least I looked respectable – though my hair was full of dust from my day in the cellar. I crept out to the main door: it had a Yale lock, opened easily from the inside. I could see no-one.

Quietly I slipped away and picked up my bike, which was still lying in the trees near the exit. Ten minutes later I was cycling away on the open road.

I was no longer afraid of the police station. These people had tried to kill me, now was time for me to speak out.

In fact the police were a lot more attentive than I had feared. I sensed that my tale was only confirming suspicions they had assembled from other sources. My story seemed to prompt action from the Inspector. He wasn't talking to me, obviously, but I was still in the room. I gathered that a raid was planned for Monday morning.

He turned to me. 'Miss Goode, it's vital they don't know you're still alive. Is there any way you can get away from here for the next few weeks?'

I started the European tour of my long vacation that very night. Two college friends were about to explore Italy and I invited myself to join them. Fortunately my handbag lived with my funeral attending gear and I had all the cards with me that I needed.

I never told anyone what had happened – not, at least, until I came to give evidence in the court later that year.

14. HATHAWAY PATH AWAY

It was a slow, rutted road back from London but the thought of seeing my lovely wife after three long years gave me energy – plus my children, of course. Though they would be bigger than the toddler and baby twins I had left behind.

'Good morrow, household,' I shouted, throwing off my mud-splattered cloak as I reached my home once again.

There was a frightening silence.

I strode into the kitchen but it looked unnaturally tidy. There were no pots waiting to be washed. The butter scoop hadn't been used for months.

I put my bag down and raced from room to room: all empty. And it had been that way, I perceived, for some time.

The neighbours must know something. And when I hailed them they were still the same. Friendly enough on the surface, like all Stratford folk, but I sensed suspicion beneath.

'You been away a long time, Will,' the husband observed. 'Anne waited so desperately for letters – she didn't even know where you'd gone . . . but none ever came. So what you been doing all these years?'

Then it hit me. I had been charged, by the highest official in the land, to tell no-one of my activity. I was proud of what I had done but I was not at liberty to explain myself – leastways, not to him.

'But where is Anne?' I burbled, '. . . and my children?'

'Ah. She said to tell you, if you ever came back, the little ones are safe with her mother. But she went off determined to follow you. London, I think she headed for first.'

He shook his head. 'That's a long road for a woman to travel alone. But your Ann, she's got some spirit, I'll give her that.'

I didn't stay even one night in Stratford. How could I while my beloved was missing? Anyway, the longer I stayed the more I would be challenged to account for my absence by Stratford burghers. I tarried only to search carefully for any plan from my beloved but none was to be found.

Within an hour I had secured a carriage heading back for London.

I had been taught investigatory skills during my training as a Crown agent - for one thing so I could detect any trace of being followed. So, given my resourceful Anne had come to London after me, what traces of me might she have found?

In 1585 I had been twenty one years old, an unknown. I had lodged for a month near the Tower of London, not even giving my full name. I was sure nothing could be gleaned there, whatever her state of desperation.

Even so, I had been nowhere else. I headed that way again.

As I approached I remembered the one-legged beggar, Stephano, with his regular patch outside the Tower. He had been seated there three years ago, when I passed daily to and from my training. You may laugh, but I had been drawn to him as another nobody in this large city, someone I could greet without incurring ridicule, condescension or contempt. As the days had gone

105

by I shared snippets of my poems, which seemed to please him. And in time Stephano took to giving me a responsive verse.

His lines did not scan but at least they did rhyme.

Stephano was still there: would he remember me? I approached him, smiling, and offered a short verse in greeting. Without hesitation he gave me a matching reply. His poetry seemed to have improved over time. Perhaps he would say the same of mine.

It was only as I started to walk on that it came to me: his reply was better than before because it was two lines I had crafted myself. He must have remembered those lines for almost three years.

I turned back to face him and tried another. Again he replied – or rather, continued my poem – at once.

Only this time there was something really odd. For the verse I had just spoken had been composed on the birth of Susanna, my first child, five years earlier, a simple sonnet dedicated to my wife. It had never been heard outside Stratford. There was only one way this man could have come across it.

I seized him roughly by the jerkin and hauled him to what was left of his feet. 'Stephano, how knowest thou this poem?'

He staggered but did not flinch, 'Sire, your wife did teach it me. Anne, she was called. She said it was in honour of your first child.'

'Huh. And what else did my wife teach you?'

'She was here last winter - six months ago. 'Twas bitter cold. She said you had left her for a season but that she would never let you go.'

'That much 'tis true. I am after her; seeking her now. Dost

thou know where she went?'

'Sire, I hast some idea. But see my state; the story must be worth a meal.'

I was under great pressure. There was no doubt I was stronger than him. It was tempting to extract whatever information he had by force.

Then I remembered our verbal jousting from years earlier. There were funds in my bag, the final payment from my years as a Crown agent. It would not harm to share a little with this beggar.

The Speckled Hen was directly opposite. I put my shoulder under his arm to help him over and seized a bench without. The bedraggled beggar looked and smelt too gross to take inside.

I realised that I too was hungry. Soon we were both gulping huge portions of broth and chunks of bread. I feared the effect of supplying him with beer but it was safer than the local water. I waited till my potential informant had satisfied his worst pangs of hunger before pressing him further.

'Stephano, I will leave funds with the landlord to buy you the same food again for this next week. First, though, tell me all you can remember of my wife's visit.'

This was obviously more than he had expected. He paused to collect his thoughts.

'Sire, she was dressed in a green woollen coat, on her own and desperate for news. She had connected you, somehow, with the Tower. Then she spotted me sitting outside and approached me. It was your poems that made the link between us. Not many speak in sonnets.'

I dimly recalled a note I had sent home, before I began my agent training and was sworn to secrecy, it might have mentioned the Tower. His tale made some kind of sense. 'So what happened next?'

'I told her that the Tower was used for training of agents before they were sent abroad.'

I stared at him. 'However did you know that?'

'All you see now, sire, is a beggar. Long ago I too was an agent but once I was interrogated I lost my strength – as well as my leg. The authorities allow me to sit outside as a favour; as well as being a special way to watch for trouble.'

'But . . . but you had no idea where I would be sent.'

'Anne told me that you spoke Italian and Spanish. Back then there was more trouble in Italy than in Spain. Queen Mary of Scots had just been executed. Anyway, that was where I had worked. You might have been my replacement.'

I nodded and he continued.

' I knew just one other Crown agent in that land. It was against everything I had ever sworn to reveal it, but I saw the distress in Anne's eyes. In the end I told her his assumed name and town. He was called Proteus and he was based in Milan.'

It was incredible that my humble, devoted wife would travel abroad in search of me but now I had a location where she might be found. My years as a Crown agent had made me used to inconspicuous travel and my funds allowed me coach passage through France. I took care, while on board, to speak only in fluent Spanish. A fortnight later I had reached the North Italian city of Milan and could start the search for Proteus.

'Twould have been impossible to find him without bringing attention on myself but for the advice of Stephano. Bless him, he had told me the tavern which Proteus most often frequented and something of his appearance. 'Tall and angular, bearded and distinguished,' I was told. It was two days later that I spotted someone that might be him and a few days more before I was certain.

I had no wish to accost Proteus inside the tavern. I knew not who else might be watching; after all, I was in enemy territory. But by the time I had thrice followed him home I knew where he lived, when he would leave the tavern and the route he would take. It was not hard for me to be lurking at the loneliest point as he strode past.

'Good night, Sire,' I addressed him in English. It was a gamble but I had no choice.

He jolted to a halt and looked hard at me. Then he glanced round to see if it was some sort of trap. It was a dark night and there was no-one else there.

'Who art thou?' He spoke in Italian but slowly; not his first language. I replied in English.

'We have never met but we are from the same place. A mutual friend in London told me your name and sent me to find you. My name is William, I am following after my wife. Did she reach here?'

But it was the mention of the friend that grabbed his attention and restored his native tongue. 'Stephano?' he gushed, 'Stephano is still alive? Thank God. The King's men dealt with him so cruelly. How is he?'

I too was aware of the hazard of speaking in English. 'Can we not talk somewhere more secure?'

'I fear, William, that I am under watch. My home has already been raided once. It is dark enough here. Let us stroll slowly and talk quickly.'

'We will talk of Stephano shortly, but first my own question: hast thou met my wife?'

His brow furrowed. 'Two months ago I met someone else sent by Stephano. A page; clean-shaven, small of stature, fair, curly hair. I took him as a man. But now you make me question . . . the voice was exceeding high.'

My scalp tingled. This was surely Anne. What enterprise - to cross Europe dressed as a pageboy. 'And what did you say to her?'

'I told her I had met no "William Shakespeare" in Milan. There was, though, another agent recently arrived in Verona - Valentine. She declared she would try to find him.'

'Do you know more?'

Proteus shrugged. 'I never saw her again. But the King's army is highly active in that town. Their interrogation is without mercy. If you follow, I beg you, take the greatest care.'

I had never heard of Verona before this moment. But his testimony was clear: my wife had gone there. There was no time to be lost. Pausing only for details of Valentine – Proteus was reluctant to tell me but I pointed out that he had already told my wife – I prepared to travel onwards.

I followed the same method in Verona as in Milan. The town was smaller but had more soldiers, based in the local Castle. After a week's preparation I contrived a midnight rowing-boat meeting with Valentine.

Once again the luckless Stephano was our common bond. I saw Valentine was not as tense as Proteus. Was this because he felt safe or just had less experience of what could go wrong? After a few moments I broached my mission: had he come across a curly-haired page with a high voice?

At once his cheerful face darkened. 'I believe she was called Anne. I never met her but I heard she once tried to find me. But before she could she fell into the hands of soldiers and was taken to the Castle. I am truly sorry, sire. Few emerge from there un-scathed. Did you have hopes of her?'

The case seemed hopeless but I was not giving up. During my preparations I had seen a poster offering jobs in the Castle. It seemed the only way to find out if Anne was still there.

I went next day. There were not many applicants. I inter-spersed my broken Italian with fluent Spanish. They could see I would understand orders, which was all they needed; they took me on at once.

For two or three days I did my best to memorise the layout of the Castle as I scurried from task to task. Then I was told to go down to the cellar to assist with an interrogation. I felt my way down the steep stairs. There were no windows in the chamber. It was almost dark, apart from the lantern over the doorway.

And then my heart stopped. For there in front of me, stretched on a long wooden rack, was a young maiden. Her head was on the far side from the doorway so I could not see her face but the howls of anguish showed that she was far gone. My task, I was told, was to help wind the torture wheel one notch at a time. Then the maiden's howls turned into repeated screams of agony as a crunching noise came from her hips.

'Tis not far to the end now,' commented the chief guard. I grasped his Italian but saw no need to respond. Indeed my emotions, as I saw my beloved being literally torn in two, would scarce let me speak.

I will not linger, dear readers, on the next hour. The maiden was full of courage. Even under immense pressure she would give nothing away (if indeed she knew anything worth telling). Finally she passed away. And at last, as I helped release the body and tidy the chamber, I saw her face – and joy of joys, the maiden was not my Anne.

As I stumbled towards the gloomy Castle door at the end of my shift my head was reeling. Was Anne still alive or had she suffered the same grisly end earlier? Was she in another cell, awaiting the same fate, maybe tomorrow? I could imagine no way to rescue her.

Suddenly, as I approached the Castle door, it opened and a cart was driven in. There were two soldiers on board but both urgently needed a pee. For a precious minute I was alone with the cart. And I saw there was someone else on board, covered by a rough blanket.

My instinct said, whatever else goes on, here is one you can rescue. I lifted the blanket and helped the person off, slung them over my shoulder and paced out through the Castle doors. I did not stop till I reached my lodgings.

And there I saw, to my astonishment and delight, that by some miracle I had rescued my beloved.

She was still dressed as a pageboy. 'Do they know you are a woman?' She shook her head.

'I have a plan,' I continued. 'Wait here.'

An hour later I returned with female garments, enough to turn my pageboy into a glamorous woman. And new clothes for myself.

We caught the next carriage for Innsbruck. Of course we were pulled in on the way but the soldiers were searching for a pageboy, not a woman of elegance. I played the proud husband to perfection. I hardly needed to act at all.

When we started again, Anne turned to me. 'Thou art a fine actor, William. 'Twould be a much safer profession than being a Crown agent.'

'Darling, I've already stopped being an agent. I was planning to write plays. I could set one in Verona. I have met two Gentlemen in these parts that warrant wider attention. A girl who dresses as a pageboy would add an unusual touch.'

The kitchen of Anne Hathaway's cottage in Stratford. As clean today as at the start of this story.

15. REFERENDUM RAG

I'd been a part-time cleaner at the Eilean Donan Castle, with its wonderful view across the Kyle of Lochalsh and over to Skye, for a long time. I'd seen some odd things over the years but nothing came close to this.

It was the start of July and I'd been asked to put in some overtime on the Banqueting Room, the largest room in the Castle. It's a majestic room with many banners and other ornaments, used for weddings and other special events – James Bond shot a scene in there once. Apparently something top secret was about to happen. It was nine o'clock on Saturday morning and for the time being the place was closed to visitors.

The main room had taken me longer than usual and I was running late. But I'd finished the room at last and was working on the narrow, hidden passageway that runs around it: it had been built to provide an extra layer of protection in far-off days, when the head of one Clan was meeting another. It's not mentioned in the Castle publicity and not many folk know it's there. The only clue to the passage that you can see from the Banqueting Room is a few tiny spy holes, which overlook the main entrance and parts of the banqueting table.

There was a banging noise like someone moving furniture or heaving equipment. Then I heard the sound of people arriving in the Banqueting Room. Of course, I didn't use the holes to see who it was. It was none of my business. But as I kept polishing the panels in the passage I couldn't help hearing what was being said; and the conversation sent shivers down my spine.

'I must say, this is a splendid setting, Nicola.'

'Och, it's by far the most photographed castle in the Highlands. One of your ancestors hid here, I believe. But it would have been a mistake, Charles, to meet anywhere near Edinburgh. Not while we were hoping for an off-the-record exchange, eh.'

Nicola's accent was Ayrshire Scottish, as crisp as you could wish. In contrast "Charles", whoever he was, sounded aristocratic English and slightly confused. What on earth were they talking about? I listened harder.

'I mean, everything is such a muddle at the moment, Nicola. This bloody referendum result for a start. And for now Westminster's got a zombie government facing a zombie opposition.'

'That's only a London perspective, Charles. Here in Scotland we're more optimistic. I see the whole thing as a great opportunity, provided it's handled correctly.'

'Oh, you mean it's the chance for another Independence vote?'

'Well, yes - ultimately. But a lot of things have to happen first.'

'I can tell you, this time you'd have my vote – except that I'm one of the few people in the country who's not allowed to express an opinion.'

There was silence for a moment. I shifted my position to try and see who was talking but they'd chosen to sit at one corner of the table that was out of vision.

I heard the sound of Nicola shuffling. She sounded impatient. 'You asked for this meeting, Charles. I'm sure we're both busy people. I've got a country to run and you, well . . .'

'Actually, I might soon be very busy. The referendum result

hit Mother very hard. Most of her staff are from overseas, I've no idea how we'd replace them with UK nationals – not at the wages we pay. And the thought of having to apply for a visa every time she wanted to see one of her fellow-royals in Europe came as a nasty shock.'

'Now I think of it, we haven't been told the Queen's reaction to the result.'

'She's not been seen outside the Palace since it was announced. In all the rumpus no-one's noticed but the sad truth is that she's collapsed. The doctor thinks she's had a stroke; he's warned me that she's not likely to last more than a few days. That's why this has to be a flying visit – I'm due back this afternoon. It's my turn to sit by her bedside. But what I wondered, Nicola, was what I could do for the Nationalist cause once I was, as it were, off the substitutes' bench and a fully active monarch?'

'Charles, I'm so sorry.' It sounded like a catch in her voice. 'Thank you for telling me. Poor old Lizzie. Mind, she's had a good run. If I'm still running Scotland when I'm ninety I won't complain. Well, I'll be as brief as I can.'

There was another pause. I put down my rag and stopped polishing altogether, making sure I was seated comfortably. I didn't want to be discovered now. Then Nicola continued.

'My problem, Charles, is with the timing. There may be a bit of a tussle with Westminster over a second Scottish referendum but it was in the SNP manifesto; I'll call it whenever I want. If some dim-witted English MPs in Westminster try to block it, that'll only help me win over Scottish voters. Trouble is, it'll only work – and deliver the result I'm after - if it's clear to Scottish folk that a vote for independence is actually the only way that they can

116

stay in Europe.'

'My dear Nicola, isn't that a given?'

There was the sound of a sigh. 'Och, Charles, you live too sheltered a life. It all depends on the sequence. If Britain gives notice to the European Union –'

'– you mean triggers Article Fifty, not just threatens to do so?'

'Yes. Then arguably any later secession by Scotland from England will mean that we will have to apply to join Europe as a new member. Our last 43 years membership as part of the UK, with all the opt-outs that we've contrived, would be set aside. We'd even have to use the wretched Euro. They'd never let us use the pound sterling. That's sinking like a stone anyway.'

'Oh. You mean it's not the *end* of the negotiations, when Britain formally leaves, that's the critical point, it's when they first give notice to quit?'

'So my lawyers tell me. Scotland's negotiations, to be allowed to stay, need to be launched before any negotiations for the rest of the UK to leave begin.'

'But . . . doesn't that mean you need to call the new Scottish referendum at once?'

'The trouble is, even if I were to call the referendum tomorrow, there would be a few months before it took place. Alex would want to tramp about again and sound like he's still in charge. There'd need to be time for speeches and election debates. The earliest time it could happen would be the autumn.'

'But I don't quite see . . . what's wrong with that?'

'Given a date, the Conservatives would make sure Article Fifty was triggered before it happened. That would make it doubtful that I could win my referendum. The Euro is pretty unpopular everywhere.'

Once again there was silence. I knew politics had become like a soap opera after the UK referendum result had been announced, with leaders' resignations and candidates' back-stabbings occurring daily. Even the opposition parties had joined in. But what I was hearing now would cap all that. This wasn't Westminster tittle tattle, it was an intelligent conversation between two people who had power to make things happen.

I made sure I was comfortable and listened hard.

'Let's assume Mother passes away in the next few days. That will make me King – even before any Coronation. "The Queen is dead: long live the King." It's a new regime: I wouldn't need to do things in the same way.'

'How d'you mean?'

'Well, everyone regards me as slightly eccentric. What they don't realise is that's just a facade. I'm going to be a lot more radical once I'm in charge. This'll be one Jacobite rebellion that succeeds.'

'Careful, Charles.' Nicola sounded worried now. 'Don't overplay your hand. The democracy we have now may be rickety but nearly all of us would say the "divine right of kings" has gone for good.'

'Don't misunderstand me, Nicola. I don't want to do away with Parliament. I just want to make sure it's tuned to the will of the people by being a more pro-active monarch.'

'Yes . . .What did you have in mind?'

'Most experts agree that it's Parliament that has to support the application of Article Fifty to trigger the exit. And the Act of Parliament in 1973, by which we joined the European Common

Market, can only be revoked by Parliament.'

'But I still don't see -'

'Well, all Acts of Parliament need the royal assent before they become law. When they brought me this one I would just refuse to sign it.'

Even Nicola, past-master of political finesse, seemed stunned by this idea.

'But Charles, that'd cause an eruption of anger – at least in England. Remember 52% of the electorate voted for "Leave". You'd never make it stick.'

'Not in the end - but it would lead to a massive delay. I'd make it clear that I would sign the bill, as soon as you'd held your own referendum here in Scotland and taken action on the result. If the Scottish people had voted for independence as a means of retaining membership of the European Union before the UK triggered its exit and had applied to remain, would that not make all the difference?'

'It might well. But you would be hugely unpopular as the English King. You might never get crowned.'

'If I'd achieved one thing that most of the people wanted I'd be happy to abdicate. Retire to Balmoral . . . or even recommission the Britannia. How would you feel about having Prince William as your next King of Scotland?'

'Well, he's got a degree from St Andrews. That's a good start.'

I guess that Charles must have glanced at his watch. 'My gosh, it's already nine thirty. I'm sorry, I need to go. My helicopter will be waiting. So that's just between the two of us for now. I'll be in touch once Mother is no longer with us.'

I heard the sound of rapid farewells and the pair heading for the exit.

Somehow having a tidy Scottish castle no longer seemed so important. This was a scoop. But what could I do? Who would ever believe me?

I finished my polishing and ventured back into the Banqueting Room. And to my astonishment came across a cameraman, busy removing a large camera.

'I heard all of that,' I told him. That didn't seem to bother him as much as I'd expected.

'Yes, it's another docu-drama about the 2016 referendum – ways it might have continued. To be broadcast later in this year. Should be very popular in some quarters.'

Eilean Donan Castle on the Kyle of Lochalsh.

16. GARDEN OF EDEN

'Darling, I've finally made it. I've got a part in this year's Mystery Play.'

I had plugged away doing amateur dramatics locally for years but never made it into professional theatre.

My husband, who had just walked through the door, grinned and gave me a hug. Then the tall legal beagle nosed down for the small print. 'Well done, Shelley. Do you know what part it'll be?'

'They're finalising it this week, I should hear shortly. It won't be long before I'm called to rehearsal.'

Chester's Mystery Plays, based on the Bible, were an annual event, taking place in the open-air ruins of the Museum Gardens in September. Trevor and I attended regularly. Each time there'd been a different visiting Director. This was by no means the first time I'd applied for a part.

The casting letter came a week later. I was to play Eve in the opening scene, based on the creation account in Genesis. It could have been worse. One year a wild woman called Jael had been featured, killing her enemies with tent pegs. Last year a young Salome had performed a no-holds-barred striptease at the court of King Herod that resulted in John the Baptist being beheaded. I had a presentable figure (or so Trevor said) but fortunately was too old for that.

As I told him, a sliver of doubt crossed Trevor's face. 'If you're lucky it might be a mild autumn. I don't suppose you'll have many clothes on.'

The question of what Eve would be wearing, in a modern version of a medieval mystery play, had not occurred to me. 'I think that, last year, Eve wore a flesh-coloured bikini. But that'll depend on how the Director wants to present it. Do we know who it is?'

'It was in this evening's paper.' Trevor retrieved it from his brief case and found the relevant page. 'It's someone called Simeon Dangerfield. That's odd. I shared rooms at College with a Simon Dangerfield who put on all sorts of plays. Google might tell us if it's the same bloke.'

After dinner I looked up Dangerfield on the internet. 'Simeon is an up and coming director from Manchester,' I reported. 'He doesn't take much notice of convention. Several of his productions have shocked the locals. He's never done a Mystery Play before. It might be good if he can shake things up a bit.'

Rehearsals started a fortnight later, ten weeks before the first performance. The organisers reckoned it was better to force the pace. I'd already been sent my script and was glad to see Eve did not have many lines.

Simeon was a long-haired, determined-looking man in his late thirties so my husband might have known him. His assistant was a drama student called Donna. There was no messing about; he had obviously thought hard about what he wanted.

'This first evening we've going to do a read-through of the whole Play. I'll make comments as we go.'

The read-through began. The Mystery Plays were based

loosely on scenes from the Bible. I was first on with Adam. The man playing this part must have been chosen for his stature and rugged appearance. In contrast, the Serpent, who came after us, seemed slimy even before he was into costume. Some care must have gone into the casting.

The three of us read the scene through. Simeon urged us to project our voices and not to rush it, then to read it again. 'This is the pivotal scene in the whole story. It sets the problem that the rest of the Bible is trying to unravel. We have to grab the audience's attention straight away.'

'These guys will be completely naked,' observed Donna. 'That should attract some attention anyway.'

For a second I thought I must have misheard. Then I glanced at Adam and saw that he was shocked as well. Was this the time to challenge Donna's assumptions? Had this plan come from Simeon? I cleared my throat. But before either of us could say anything the Director had moved on to scene two.

At the end of the evening Simeon gave us encouragement for our first efforts and a challenge for the days ahead. 'We'll be doing three rehearsals a week, here in the Museum Gardens – whatever the weather. By the end of week two I want you all to know your lines. And for the last fortnight we'll rehearse in costume.'

Was it my imagination or was he giving me an evil grin?

I reached home in a panic. 'Trevor, it's all going horribly wrong.'

'You've only had one rehearsal, Shelley. It can't be that bad.'

I swallowed and then confessed. 'They're expecting me to play the part of Eve completely naked. What am I going to do?'

My lovely Trevor scooped me up into his arms and gave me an intense hug. 'I did wonder, you know. Does Simeon want to restore the style of the first performance?'

'But they didn't do it stark naked in Medieval times.'

'No, no, I meant the first Garden of Eden. If the story is accurate they must have been naked then.'

'I've never ever been naked in public. Or even topless.'

'Darling, let's take this slowly. The way you've learned this has come as a nasty shock. But suppose that the part was advertised from the start as "Eve: to be enacted nude". Might you still have applied, even knowing that? Especially if that was the only part on offer?'

I thought for a moment. 'I was pretty desperate. I suppose I might have done – provided you were OK about it.'

Trevor smiled. 'It's not as though it's erotic nakedness to boost sales. It's a religious play. You could consider it a great honour to have been assigned the part – the world's first full woman.'

'Darling, I'll make it up to you afterwards. If every man in Chester has seen me naked I'll make sure you're not forgotten.'

Trevor looked happy. I was sure he wouldn't let me forget those words.

Rehearsals continued. Simeon had some distinctive ideas. It was going to be an edgier production than usual. I comforted myself that my opening scene was quite short. It would be swamped in the audience's memory by later effects. They would remember Salome's performance long after mine.

We came to the rehearsals "in costume". By now the sets had been constructed.

'What's this deep pool of water over here?' I asked Simeon.

'I thought it would be a good idea for you to hide there beforehand and then emerge from it. Even with today's NHS I doubt you can be brought straight out of the body of Adam.'

'But will it be heated?'

He looked at me with amazement. 'Darling, they didn't have heating in the Garden of Eden. Don't worry; you won't be in for more than twenty minutes.'

It was far too late to start arguing. It occurred to me, as I waited in the icy water, that they wouldn't have towels in the Garden either. So once I got out I would have to act the whole scene dripping wet. I would be very cold indeed. And when we finally came to perform, it certainly was. The only positive feature was that my shivering blocked out most of my embarrassment at being naked.

Later I expressed my anguish to Trevor.

'I've been doing some background checks,' he replied. 'Your Simeon Dangerfield was my Simon. And I was reminded of more of his antics. He contrived every year to put on a play in which one or two girls had to appear naked on the College terrace. There were suspicions that his interests went a lot deeper. I don't know exactly what happened but he was sent down – never completed the course. I'm still waiting on enquiries about his later career. So you've reason to be worried. No wonder he's modified his name.'

If the same thing was happening here I could guess who the other victims might be. I arranged with Donna and the girl playing Salome to meet at a local café before the next rehearsal. 'My husband Trevor once shared rooms with Simeon,' I began.

'He was sent down for high jinks with girls in the end-of-year plays he put on. All he's done with me so far is to make me act naked and very cold. Has he tried anything with either of you?'

It turned out he had. Salome had been given intimate coaching on her sensuous dance and Donna had been given no choice but to share his hotel room. Each had assumed they were in a special relationship. They were very angry to learn that Simeon had form on this, going back a long, long way.

'But what are going to do?' asked Donna. 'Simeon is a well-regarded Director. If we complain he'll just brush us aside.'

So I explained my plan.

It was on the evening of the first performance that a call came in from Adam. 'Sorry folks. I've been in a car crash. I fear I've broken my leg.'

Donna turned to the Director. 'Simeon, we can't train up anyone new at this stage. You'll have to play the part. I'm sure you'll do it very well.' Others made similar noises and Simeon realised he had little choice. Most of the cast were keen to see him coping with the evening cold as he had made them do - especially as the late Indian summer now seemed to be over.

I made one or two special preparations and then, gritting my teeth, climbed into the pool. Simeon had insisted I was in the water well before the audience started to arrive.

The lights were dimmed and the drama began. Simeon (the new Adam), completely naked, strode across the grass and had a conversation with the invisible God, culminating in a cry of anguish at being alone.

'Lie down,' came a voice from the sky, 'and I will bring forth a

126

companion for you.'

Simeon duly lay down. I had strewn one or two objects carefully around the grass so the only space he could lay was beside the pool.

Quietly I crept out on the other side and tiptoed round until I stood behind him.

'For years, Simeon, you have made others suffer. Now it is your turn,' I yelled. And leaning forward, I rolled him into the pool.

The water was especially cold that evening. For as part of the plan Salome had ordered two large buckets of ice from the local fishmonger; I had tipped them in as I started my evening. The water was extremely cold but I was hardened from the last fortnight's rehearsals.

Simeon, though, was not acclimatised at all. He howled in shock and rage.

The audience was bemused. They had been warned to expect an edgy performance: was this it? At once I dived in again and dragged him down to the bottom.

Then all at once there were three Eves. Salome and Donna, also naked, had joined me and between us we held him down.

It was preferable that he did not drown. But by the time we let go he was not in much of a position to argue. He lay slumped, coughing and spewing out water, at the edge of the pool.

'Ladies and gentlemen,' I began. I was still naked but now I was not ashamed. I felt this gave me more authority. 'What you have just seen is a variant on the traditional Mystery Play. This is a modern take on the Garden of Eden. Simeon Dangerfield here,' I gestured towards him, 'has for years exploited women in the plays he has directed. It all began at University, from which he was eventually expelled. My husband is putting out a detailed press release as I speak.

'Later,' I went on, 'there were a series of incidents around the country. In each case Simeon's reputation kept him safe against the word of unknown actresses. Tonight you have seen three of us, his latest victims, combine to bring him down.'

'The Garden of Eden,' I went on, 'is a tale of temptation, yielding and consequence. The rest of this Play is about trying to redress that failure. But tonight's scene one is different; here a source of evil has been challenged and exposed. And if there is any justice in the world, if the authorities are listening, this man will never, ever, be allowed to maltreat women again.'

17. ONE FOOT IN THE GRAVE

The phone call had come as a nasty shock.

'Mr Sadnicki?'

'Yes?' This sounded horribly like a cold caller. Was I about to be told about a recent accident involving my car?

'Mr James Sadnicki?'

'That's right.' It might be a cold caller but they'd got my full name. 'What's the matter?'

'I'm ringing from the Waitrose car park in Wallingford. It's about your Dad - William. I'm afraid he's had a fall. We called an ambulance. They were very thorough but he was as white as a sheet – hardly conscious. They've just rushed him to hospital.'

I swallowed hard. 'Thank you so much for telling me. I'll be there as soon as I can.'

I slammed down the phone and rushed outside to my car. Poor old Dad: I had to be at A&E.

It was only as I reached the Wallingford roundabout, on the Oxford to Reading road, that it occurred to me there was doubt on which hospital my Dad might have been taken to. The caller would have known, no doubt, if I'd thought to ask; I cursed my impatience. I'd never been good at planning.

It would probably be Oxford. I turned left and hoped traffic would be light in mid afternoon. As I drove I sadly recalled our last meeting, only two days earlier.

It was a pity he'd stalked out of my house in such a blaze; but that was Dad. All over some careless remark I made about his new Carer being "too zealous". An only child, my Mum used to say I'd inherited his temper. Sometimes she even claimed I'd made it worse. While she was alive she sometimes despaired of both of us.

How I wished I'd spoken more carefully. I didn't want our last ever meeting to be a row.

As I drove I started thinking of the good things my Dad had done for me. I recalled how he'd made sure I got a good apprenticeship in the local garage. That had been fine until I lost my temper with a wealthy customer. It was my fault that had fizzled out, not his.

Even so, he'd backed me again when I wanted to start as a technician at the local water research offices. That had gone better, actually: I was still there.

And he had looked after my Mum so well when she'd had her stroke. Taken on all the shopping and cooking and then, after her second stroke, managed to move her to a Care Home for her final days.

Dear old Dad. Was it now his turn? I found I was battling back tears as I continued to drive.

Half an hour's hectic driving later, I reached the John Radcliffe Hospital. I abandoned the car on double yellow lines and rushed inside.

'I believe my Dad – Bill Sadnicki - was brought here by ambulance earlier this afternoon. He'd had a fall while he was out shopping in Wallingford.'

The receptionist could see I was distraught but she could only deal with the facts on her computer. She interrogated it for a minute.

'I'm sorry, sir, there's no record of anyone of that name here at present. But if he arrived in the last half hour it wouldn't be on here yet. Why don't you go and have a coffee while you wait?'

I followed her advice, though it took me a while to find the cafeteria and the coffee wasn't great. Or maybe I wasn't in the mood to appreciate it.

Fifteen minutes later I was back at the desk. But there was still no sign of my Dad. 'Are you sure it was this hospital he was brought to?' she asked. 'I mean, Wallingford is slightly nearer to Reading.'

I'd guessed the wrong hospital. I rushed outside, just in time to confront the traffic warden, but not soon enough to avoid driving away with a parking ticket.

Then it was a nail-biting trip back to Reading. The evening rush-hour was beginning and it took me an hour and a half to reach the reception at the Royal Berks. But to my dismay there was no record of my Dad being brought in here either.

Why couldn't the silly fool go where I could find him? I thought. Then remembered it was entirely my fault I hadn't asked the proper question.

'Is there anywhere else he might have been taken?' I pleaded. I was desperate now.

'Depends on the ambulance, sir, and the queues at each hospital. But it sounds, from what you say, that your Dad would need somewhere substantial. The only other place they might have gone to from Wallingford would be Newbury.'

Once more I rushed back to my car and over to Newbury. Surely this would be the end of the trail?

Of course, it wasn't. Newbury had no Sadnicki either. I had another coffee and took stock.

Was this all a false alarm? Had my Dad persuaded a mate to give me the disturbing call just to get back at me for our last row? It would be a nasty trick, to say the least. I recalled, though, how cross he'd been with me when we'd last met. Arguably it would be no more than I deserved.

I braced myself and rang Dad's number: no reply. But if it was all a false alarm then he might not answer anyway. The only way to be sure was to go to his sheltered accommodation in Wallingford and see if he was there; or, if not, to check if anyone there knew where he was.

By the time I reached Dad's Home I was almost beside myself. Dad had talked gloomily, only a fortnight ago, about early dementia: surely it couldn't have progressed that quickly?

I was surprised how few people were around. Eventually I got hold of the Home Manager. 'I'm after my Dad,' I explained. 'I had an odd phone call about him earlier today.'

'Sorry James, I haven't seen him. He's probably out with the others at the Christmas Dinner.'

'Where's that?'

'It's in the White Hart –that's in the town square. We have a bus to take them down and bring 'em all back so they can drink as much as they like.'

132

He glanced at the clock. 'They'll be home by ten – that's past most of their bed times. Wait in the lounge if you like.'

I was tempted to go and find Dad in the White Hart but I didn't want a public row. It sounded likely that he was alright. Relaxing slightly, I became aware of a fierce hunger. I'd treat myself to a meal at the pub across the road and make sure I was back by ten.

The meal turned out well. Steak and chips followed by three scoops of ice cream for dessert. I started to feel rather better.

Even so, as you can imagine, it was a massive relief to see my Dad tottering off the bus with his mates two hours later. After all, I had spent the afternoon thinking I might never see him again.

I walked over and gave him a massive hug.

He blinked, looked surprised. 'Jim, it's good to see you. What brings you over?'

'Dad, I had a phone call this afternoon to say you'd collapsed in the car park and been taken to hospital. I've spent the whole afternoon trying to find you. Thank goodness you're alright.'

'Never felt better, son. Mind, my friend, Bert, had a turn when we went shopping this afternoon. They called an ambulance for him. Maybe there was some muddle over which of us was injured?'

That made some sort of sense, I suppose.

It was as I drove home half an hour later that it occurred to me it might all be rather more than "a muddle". I'd left my house in a rush and been away since three – that was eight hours ago. It had been daylight when I left and I hadn't bothered putting on lights. I expected that uniquely, on our Close, my place would be in pitch darkness.

But as I drove in, I saw it was in darkness no longer. Every light in the house was blazing and the front door was ajar. Horrified, I rushed in to see what had happened.

There was no-one there now, at any rate. As far as I could see nothing had been stolen. But it was a nasty surprise. I thought of calling the police but what could I tell them? I could imagine them saying, 'You say you left home in a hurry, sir? Maybe you didn't lock it at all?'

Next morning, feeling a mixture of contrition and anger, I headed back to my Dad's. Was there something he wasn't telling me?

I offered to take him out to lunch and had another excellent meal at the pub opposite. It was a good opening move – I should do this more often. We talked and talked; eventually I got to his understanding of the truth.

Dad admitted that had told Bert, in front of his Carer, about our row two days ago and how upset it had made him.

Bert's collapse in Wallingford market was unplanned. But it had given an opportunity for retaliation. So (my Dad assumed) Bert must have given Dad's name, not his own, to a passer-by: it was a way to pay me back.

Bert had been quickly seen at the hospital and sent home.

Once home Bert must have rung my house and found I was still out, guessed where I might be. So as a further act of revenge, he'd gone round to my house, turned on the illuminations and left the door ajar.

It was a series of nasty tricks but I knew I had upset Dad badly. It sounded almost plausible. Just a few details needed checking.

'Dad, how did Bert get hold of the keys to my house?'

'You know, I'm not sure, son. I have a set for emergencies but they keep 'em in the Home's office.'

'The thing that I find really hard to believe, Dad, is that someone about to get in an ambulance, feeling really ill, would dream of giving a false name to a passer-by. Do you really think Bert could be that devious?'

A pause. 'You know, son, you might be right. He's an honest sort of bloke. But if it wasn't him . . ?'

I took a deep breath.

'Please don't be mad, but it seems to me the obvious person to consider is your Carer. I mean, he knew about the row – and that it involved me being rude about him in the first place. And he could access the key to my house from the Home's office.'

Dad drew breath and mused on what I had just said.

'I think you said my Carer was too zealous. You know, maybe you're right. I'll keep a closer eye on him in the future.'

'But whoever it was, and whatever they were aiming for, it's brought the two of us closer together,' said Dad, smiling. And this time I had no wish to disagree.

18. SCOOP

The Hawker Hunter hurtled over Middle Wallop airfield and began to climb – the first stage of a spectacular loop. Higher and higher, till it was but a speck in the clear blue sky; then, with the crowds below straining their necks to watch, the jet levelled out and started a shrieking descent.

Standing in the crowd, teenager Robbie Glendenning sensed all was not well. He'd attended air shows before at Middle Wallop, in the summer holidays, and knew what to expect.

'That trajectory's far too steep,' he observed to his friend. 'The pilot can't intend to swoop that low?'

He was glad to see the plane wasn't heading for the crowd but for some leafy oaks on the far side of the airfield: but it was cutting things very fine - very fine indeed.

Then, horror of horrors, the plane did not pull out of the dive but continued straight into the wood. A fireball erupted and, a few seconds later, came the sound of a massive explosion. For an instant the crowd were stilled into a shocked silence.

Then, as warning bells rang and the airfield fire engines started to race towards the blaze, a chorus of shouts and distress cries arose from the spectators. But for the pilot it was all far too late. Robbie had seen that he hadn't managed to eject; he would surely not survive the crash.

It took several hours for Robbie and his pal to get home. The air show was declared "over" within minutes but the result was exit-traffic overload. By the time they'd reached Andover the two had gone over the events again and again; but there were far more questions than answers.

Robbie's parents had watched the accident on the early evening news but weren't in a position to answer any of them.

Over the next few days came a series of bland statements from those in authority. No-one would say anything before the Air Accident Investigation Branch had reported; but Robbie had seen the explosion and doubted there would be much left to investigate.

The youngster was halfway through sixth form, had time on his hands and spent much of it the public library. It was August; the politicians were abroad; even Mrs Thatcher was keeping her head down. Arthur Scargill's miners' strike was grinding on but it couldn't make the news every day. The broadsheets welcomed the chance to investigate something different and Robbie became an avid reader. He'd never bothered with newspapers before and was surprised they could be so incisive.

He learned that the aircraft involved was too old to have a "black box" to record flight details. That left him wondering what the Accident Branch would be doing.

In the absence of hard facts, speculation mounted. The dead pilot had swapped with a colleague at the last minute. This was dismissed as routine but Robbie wondered why the swap had occurred; and who the lucky pilot was that had escaped the ferocious flames.

As a summer project he set himself to find out who and why.

Careful reading of the newspapers told him that the pilot had been in the RAF and based at Wittering – a small town on the far side of the country, somewhere near Peterborough. For a while he was stumped.

This was Robbie's first experience of real research. He'd done history projects for his A-levels but that had been just delving in the local library. He had no direct link with the RAF but could he manufacture an indirect one? He mused on the question for a couple of days; then remembered that his school operated a Combined Cadet Force for its more bloodthirsty students. One of the teachers in charge, Peter Johnson, used to have links with the RAF: maybe he could suggest a way for his student to find out more?

His school was surprised to see the student in the holidays but supportive of his project. He wheedled Johnson's phone number from the school bursar. Two days later he was invited to visit him for a fact-finding encounter.

Peter Johnson was very interested in Robbie's first-hand account of the crash at Middle Wallop. It turned out he had taken part in air displays for a few years himself, before moving into teaching.

'Why did you give it up, sir?'

'To be honest, Robbie, I got scared. The planes were getting older and older. I could see that sooner or later something would go wrong. I didn't want to be the one in charge when it did.'

'So your guess would be that it was a mechanical fault that downed the plane at Middle Wallop?'

'Probably, lad. They're very complicated machines, you see, modern aeroplanes. And air displays push them close to their limits. If something goes wrong there's not much the pilot can do – apart from doing their best to avoid crashing onto the crowds.'

'I read, sir, that the dead pilot had swapped with a colleague at the last minute. I was wondering if I could meet the man he swapped with. They're all based at RAF Wittering.'

'Well, well. That was my last posting. Let me make a few phone calls. I'll see if I can find out his name; leave it with me.'

Two evenings later the Glendenning's phone rang and his dad answered.

'It's your physics teacher, Robbie. He says he wants to talk to you about extra homework.'

Robbie seized the phone as his dad, slightly puzzled, slipped back into the kitchen.

'Hi, Robbie. It took me a while but I've managed to find out the name of the lucky pilot. He's called Max Williams. He'd love to meet you and hear an eye-witness account of what happened at Middle Wallop. The whole station's very cut up about it, of course. He's invited us to visit the day after tomorrow – I managed to include myself in the invitation so I can drive us over. Is that OK?'

'That's great, sir. Thank you very much.' Johnson would pick Robbie up at 9.30 so they would reach the RAF base just after lunch.

Robbie took the opportunity, on the journey, to learn as much as he could from Peter Johnson about life as a display pilot and also the setup at RAF Wittering.

One aspect that might be important, Robbie thought, was

keeping the planes airworthy. 'Who does the plane maintenance at the base?' he asked.

'In my day the maintenance men were all in the RAF. But the Tories are aiming to reduce the size and cost of the public sector. So now the work is what they call "outsourced" to civilians. They're mostly the same people, I think – they live in Wittering and there's no other engineering work - but now they're paid much smaller salaries.'

'And where does that money come from?'

'Some from the government; some is earned from the air displays the squadron does over the summer. Either way there's not as much cash as there should be. I gather, from my phone calls so far, that there's plenty of tension on the base.'

Robbie was fascinated to learn that there were so many layers to every problem. 'So RAF Wittering put on several air displays?'

'They have done in the past. Whether they will after the accident at Middle Wallop remains to be seen.'

Max Williams, when they met him, was a fit-looking man in his forties with a trim beard, keen to learn about what had happened at Middle Wallop. Robbie gave him a detailed account of the crash and he looked very distressed.

'Why did you swap with the other pilot, sir?'

'We pilots swap duties all the time, Robbie. The next display will be in Bournemouth, you see, and that's where my sister lives. It'll give me a chance to see her. Whereas none of us have family near Middle Wallop – it's miles from anywhere, as no doubt you know.'

It sounded convincing. Robbie's ideas of a secret grudge

between the pair, or competition over a local girl, looked fanciful. Peter Johnson took up the questioning.

'Robbie and I were talking on the way over about aircraft maintenance. If anything was to go wrong with a Hawker Hunter, to cause a crash like Middle Wallop, what d'you think it might be?'

'Peter, we've been round and round that, as you can imagine. A major failure would do it. If the control wire to the ailerons were to sheer in flight, for example, the pilot would have no way to pull out of the dive. But that's pretty unlikely - unless it had been nearly cut through beforehand.'

Robbie had thought about this as well. 'It looked to me as though the pilot didn't go quite high enough. Could anything have happened to his altimeter to confuse him?'

'I doubt it. Tell you what, I'll show you the hanger where we take care of the planes and let you see its instrument panel. Then you can judge for yourselves.'

Max was obviously keen to show off his aviation world. As they walked across the airfield, he and Peter compared details of life in the RAF today with life as it had been ten years earlier. Robbie kept quiet and picked up as much as he could – but it did not sound an attractive career option.

Soon they reached the hanger. There were half a dozen fighter jets inside, several with work in progress. 'As you can see,' Max said, 'we're checking everything we can.'

He led them to a Hawker Hunter. 'This is a twin of the plane you saw crash, Robbie.'

Some work was going on and there happened to be steps arranged up to the cockpit; the pilot led them up so they could peer inside the Perspex.

Max pointed. 'There's the instrument panel. Maintenance only takes it apart at major overhauls so we don't see behind it very often. The altimeter is that dial over on the top right.'

'Have I remembered right, that works by measuring change in air pressure as the plane climbs?' asked Peter Johnson. Robbie could see why he was now a physics teacher.

'That's right. The pilot initialises the meter on the runway at the start of the flight. It then measures the pressure drop as he takes off and converts that to altitude.'

'What would happen if he forgot to set it?'

'Oh, he wouldn't: it's a routine procedure. But if he did, the default is a typical day at sea level.'

Max continued to show them other details of the hanger. After another hour it was time to leave.

On the way back Robbie was still keen to make the most of the chance to talk to someone with technical expertise. Physics was more useful than he'd realised.

'Is there any way that the altimeter could be sabotaged so that the zeroing doesn't work?'

'Why on earth are you wondering that?'

'Well, Middle Wallop is well inland – several hundred feet above sea-level. So if the altimeter wasn't zeroed properly the pilot would think he was higher than he really was.'

The teacher mused for a second. 'I suppose that, on a complete overhaul, a local technician could put some radio-control device inside that could disconnect the zeroing. If they did, from what Max told us, it doesn't sound as though it would be spotted for a while.'

'If it was hidden, it could have been put in some time ago. How big a radio control transmitter would you need to activate it?'

'Oh, not too big – the size of a shoe box, say. Plus a three foot aerial.'

'Ah - so you couldn't do it discreetly?'

Johnson thought for a moment. 'It'd be obvious if you were standing in the crowd. But it'd be easy enough to do while sitting inside a car on the airfield during the actual display.'

He glanced shrewdly at the youngster. 'Are you thinking that the accident might all be the work of a highly-demotivated maintenance man?'

'What I was thinking, sir, is that I'd like to go to the next air display at Bournemouth. The trouble is, it'd be a long way on my bicycle.' He looked optimistically at his mentor.

Two weeks later Robbie and Peter Johnson drove down to Bournemouth for the air show. There had been no further news on Middle Wallop. The sense in the media was that it was just a one-off accident.

Peter Johnson had been busy checking the range and capability of modern radio control. He'd also found an article on the design of the Hawker Hunter altimeter in the technical press. It looked as though it was a viable way of causing a massive accident. But they had not a scintilla of proof that such a thing had happened.

Even so, he made sure he had a way of reaching the Control Tower.

Robbie had kept in touch with Max Williams. As the man

143

who would be flying the next display, he was ready for any ideas that might avoid a problem. Max recalled a time, three months ago, when half a dozen of the most disruptive ground staff had been given notice. It was unorthodox but it had prompted Max to take a receptive Personnel lady out for a meal. As a result she'd passed over the make and car registration number of each sacked man.

Peter ensured they arrived at the air show early and he parked with a good view of the entrance. The teacher waited on watch while Robbie checked that none of the other early arrival cars was on the short list. Then the pair took it in turns to check new arrivals while the other took time to enjoy the show.

Three hours later it all looked to have been a complete waste of time. The Hawker Hunter was due to perform in ten minutes and there was no sign of anyone from Wittering in the car park.

If someone intent on mischief was coming at all they'd be here by now. Robbie and Peter decided they might as well watch the display. The pair walked steadily towards the crowds assembled beside the runway. In the background they could hear the roar of the aerobatic jet starting to throttle up.

They'd almost reached the crowd when Robbie spotted a small black van with the label 'Wittering Welders' on the back. It might be just a coincidence but it was a long way to come. And surprisingly, given he'd come down for the display, the driver was still inside.

What should they do? In all their plans the pair had not firmed up a response: they had never envisaged that the discovery of a plausible suspect would happen so close to the time of flight.

'I'll go to the Control Tower,' said Peter. 'I'll try and warn

Max not to cut things too fine.'

As he dashed off Robbie eyed the van from behind. How to stop it getting away? Quietly he crept up on the passenger side, unscrewed the rear tyre cap and, with the aid of his penknife, pressed in the valve. A hiss as the air started to escape. He was glad that the noise was masked by the sound of the jet as it trundled to the end of the runway.

The tyre was nearly flat but the air was taking its time. He'd been holding the valve for several minutes. Robbie was suddenly aware of a pair of steel-capped boots in front of his eyes. The driver had come out to watch the display; and was not pleased to find his van being immobilised.

Before Robbie could shout for help a boot landed on his chest. As he fell to the ground further kicks followed to more sensitive areas of his body.

'Oi,' bellowed Peter, seeing what was happening as he rushed back from the Control Tower.

He flung himself at the van driver and the two fell to the ground. The crowd was useless: they were focused on the jet, now accelerating down the runway. But the school teacher had brought a policeman trudging along behind him. And Robbie, pulling himself up, shook his head groggily and joined in the fray.

A few minutes later the van driver was arrested and his hands cuffed. Robbie and Peter glanced inside the vehicle and at the electronic tangle it contained, including an aerial. The affair was now in police hands; but it looked like they had been right.

But what would happen to Max in the skies above? Had the van driver sent a signal to the plane and what would be its effect?

And had Peter's late Control Tower warning got through; and

would it be heeded? There was nothing else they could do; now they could only watch and wait.

The Hawker Hunter soared into the sky and circled the airport. It did a series of rolls then a low pass across the airfield. Red and blue smoke came from the wings as the display went on.

Finally the jet started on the steep climb that, Robbie knew, preceded the spectacular dive. The plane flew higher and higher then it levelled out and started to descend. Down and down it came and then started to come out of the dive. But the trajectory was higher than Robbie had seen at Middle Wallop. The plane wasn't far above the trees but it was above them. It was going to be all right.

Later, as they drove back to Andover, bruised but exhilarated, Robbie realised that he had enjoyed this taste of investigative journalism. He'd look into it again once he'd been to University.

If you want to read of later investigations by journalist Robbie Glendenning, he features in some of the Cornish Conundrums. For his biggest contributions so far, see Looe's Connections or Tunnel Vision.

19. BEST SERVED COLD

This would be my second croquet match of the week. Honest, I wouldn't have been there for either but for my best friend Fiona. By the way I'm Christine and we term ourselves "ladies who lunch". We meet every other Friday in the park, the Cheltenham Bandstand Café, for a leisurely lunch. Along with a few others, when their child-minders allow them out.

'It's a local competition,' said Fiona, 'centred round the residents of Walcombe Manor, but open to anyone in Cheltenham. The same bloke's won it for years. He told me they were desperate for new blood.'

'I've never seen a game of croquet, Fiona. Never even read about it, except in "Alice in Wonderland", when they used playing cards to make the hoops. I've no idea what I'll be watching.'

'I need a friend among the spectators, Christine. Please. You'll soon pick it up, it's a cross between golf and snooker.'

I'd never watched those games either, but I had seen them on TV. And Fiona sounded so desperate.

Walcombe Manor turned out to be a large house with a big garden in the leafy suburbs, a sort of upmarket Old People's Home with high security. Fiona and I arrived together. She was wearing a plain top and flared trousers, a change from her usual mini skirt. 'That's so I can swing the mallet between my legs,' she explained. I hadn't realised the game would limit what you could wear.

We weren't let in through the house but via a side gate, by a man in uniform who laboriously wrote down our names. There were other visitors too, neighbours from down the road.

The croquet lawn was larger than I'd imagined, as big as a court at Wimbledon, but with a pronounced camber. Fiona told me afterwards that it had been designed for crown bowls. Beyond the lawn was an extensive flowerbed and vegetable garden, plus a large greenhouse. A high laurel hedge surrounded the whole garden, with an iron gate on one side.

Fiona had already told me, 'This is the Final. I've wiped out two of the inmates in earlier rounds.'

The trophy, a silver sugar scoop, sat resplendent on a cloth-covered table waiting to be awarded. Last year's champion – I gathered he was called Jeremy - was already limbering up, knocking different coloured balls up and down the lawn with a massive mallet. I was relieved it wasn't a giant flamingo.

There was a small crowd of spectators, neighbours or residents at the Home. I was the only lunch lady, in fact no-one else was under sixty. I could see why they needed new blood. Jeremy had only one supporter, a rather grumpy friend from the Manor.

A coin was tossed and the game began.

Fiona had explained that you had to "run" all six hoops in turn with each ball, so I expected they'd start aiming for the first one. But no. Jeremy hit his blue to the far end of the lawn and Fiona whacked her red to the far side. There was some sort of strategy here. I asked a fellow-spectator what it was.

'They don't like to put their balls close to their opponent's because they might be "roqueted",' they explained. It sounded very painful. I decided I'd wait before asking for more information.

This game of cat and mouse went on for some time, no hoops run at all. I found it very tedious. I sensed, though, that Fiona and Jeremy were quite well matched.

Then Fiona's mallet caught in her flares and caused her to fluff her shot. Her red ball went off line and far too close to Jeremy's blue.

He pounced. 'Now you'll see a roquet,' my neighbour whispered.

Jeremy aimed his blue gently at Fiona's red. It was only a few feet away and an easy target. Then he picked his ball up and nestled the two together, after which he gave his blue a mighty blow. This sent red almost off the court at the far end and the blue up towards his other ball, which was black.

This was a much fiercer game than I had imagined.

That wasn't even the end of his turn. Now he could "roquet" the black and arrange the two so he could hit the pair over towards the first hoop. Black went the wrong side but blue finished just in front.

'He's got one more free shot,' my confidant whispered.

Which was all he needed. Jeremy used that to send blue through the hoop, after which he could roquet the black again. And so on and on and on.

You get the general idea anyway. I could see why it was like snooker. Just as boring but could take even longer.

I expected Fiona would be devastated by Jeremy's skill but she wasn't. Being ruthless was apparently what made people play croquet. I hadn't realised she had such a vicious streak.

Ten minutes later Jeremy's turn finally ended and it was Fiona's go. She essayed a massive shot across the lawn with her red, aiming at yellow; and aided by the camber, managed to flick it as her ball went past. The red thundered on to the flowerbed and felled a tall red hot poker but that didn't seem to worry her; she picked it up and completed her roquet.

A quarter of an hour later, when Fiona's turn finally ended, she was now one hoop ahead.

All went well, the battle even, until the altercations began.

Jeremy's black lay next to the hoop and he hit the ball hard towards it.

'Hey, that's a foul shot,' shouted Fiona. 'You can't swing the mallet so it disturbs the hoop.'

Jeremy looked ruffled. He was normally the self-appointed arbiter in games at the Manor. 'I've never heard that rule before.'

'Ring the Croquet Association. I've had rulings off them regularly.' Fiona offered him her phone but he declined.

'It doesn't matter, my dear, you're probably right. So what happens now?'

After some discussion the balls were all placed in their previous positions. Jeremy, though, looked upset. I hoped Fiona wouldn't give him scope for revenge.

From now on there were two games going on, a physical game of croquet and psychological mind warfare. The spirit in which the match was being played plummeted.

By now they had been playing for well over an hour. 'Can I use the loo?' asked Fiona.

'We have a rule here at the Manor that contestants must stay on court till the game's over,' he replied. I suspected it was a rule he'd just made up but Fiona wasn't in a position to argue. She looked uncomfortable but the game carried on.

Was Jeremy having second thoughts about opening up the game to a younger generation?

Finally came the bust up. Jeremy performed some act or other with his mallet that Fiona declared was a subtle form of cheating.

'I'm not bloody cheating,' he bellowed and swung hard at the blue in frustration. The timing of the stroke was exquisite. The ball flew into the air and down towards the greenhouse. There was a massive tinkling of glass.

An irate gardener appeared from his shed down the garden. But before he could reach us, the iron gate opened and a neighbour appeared. She was smartly dressed in a tweed suit and had an air of authority.

'Jeremy, what on earth are you doing?'

Fiona's competitor looked shaken. 'Dame Carol, how good to see you. This is the final of the Walcombe Manor croquet competition. I don't think you've made it before.' He gave a dry laugh. 'Fiona and I were having quite a tussle.'

'I wouldn't call it a tussle, Jeremy,' she replied. 'I've been watching from my study window. I'd call it an old man losing his temper. Unforgivably, I'd say. A poor example to the younger generation.'

She waved in my direction and then continued.

'And what's even worse, making a massive din in the process. People who buy these houses do so hoping to get away from hustle and bustle. I'm doing some work for the government and I need peace and quiet. You people'd make less noise playing five-a-side hockey!'

It was quite a tirade. I'd never heard of Dame Carol but she certainly looked the part. She even seemed to know her croquet – maybe Higher Civil Servants were taught the game on their training days.

For before Jeremy could respond, she stepped forward and started rearranging the balls from all four sides of the court. Then she seized his mallet and gave us all a lecture on the finer detail that Fiona had complained about. I didn't understand but I gathered that Fiona had been correct and Jeremy was once again in error.

She was pausing for breath as the gardener intervened. 'I recall the last time you broke my greenhouse, Mr Jeremy. We agreed that you would stop playing the game altogether until it had been repaired. That took several days.'

Dame Carol nodded. 'Quite. Maybe on another day Jeremy might be in a better mood.' And with that she turned and stomped off back through the gate.

There was silence in the garden of the Manor. No-one knew quite what to say. Until there was a howl of anguish from the house next door.

That had been Tuesday. It was agreed the final would be replayed on the Thursday and Jeremy would use the day in between to arrange replacement of the glass he had broken.

On Wednesday I caught an item of local news on Gloucestershire Radio. Police were investigating a burglary at the home of Dame Carol Evans. Government papers had been stolen. The theft had apparently taken place the previous afternoon – the afternoon of the croquet.

Was that what the howl had been all about?

Later I was rung up by the police. 'We want to reconstruct events at Walcombe Manor from Tuesday,' the Inpector said. 'We understand you were there as a spectator?'

I agreed. I remembered they'd checked us all in at the start.

'Could you attend as a spectator again tomorrow, please?'

He asked politely but it was an order, not a request. I had been wondering if Fiona would want me there again but now I had no choice. I resolved, though, that this would be the last game of croquet I would ever attend.

Fiona and I turned up at much the same time on Thursday. This time, maybe as a mark of protest, Fiona was wearing a short white dress, much more striking. The same crowd were there, with the addition of a woman police constable to watch the events unfold.

The game began as before. Jeremy was doing his best to be courteous and the game was played in a better spirit. Then they started to role-play the altercations.

Glancing up at the house next door, I could see Dame Carol watching from an upstairs window, a policeman standing behind her.

Jeremy must have agreed with the police that there was no need to break the greenhouse windows again. The reconstruction did no need to go that far. But he still shouted in frustration as he hit his ball off the lawn and well down the garden.

On cue, Carol appeared at the iron gate. The policewoman glancing at her watch, to time how long she spent in the Manor garden and away from her study.

Carol told off Jeremy once again, though we could all sense this time it wasn't for real. She also collected the balls from the various parts of the garden and explained how they should be rearranged. She also had a short conversation with Fiona. That all took longer than I had remembered. Finally she went back home. A minute later we all heard a howl of simulated anger.

After that we were each interviewed by the police. Was there anything we had seen that was different from the events on Tuesday? As far as I was concerned, I said, it was all exactly the same.

It was at the Bandstand, two weeks later, that I finally learned the truth.

'A couple of things had changed, Fiona, but I only thought of them afterwards,' I began, slightly hesitant. After all, we'd been friends for years.

'Go on.'

'Well, on Tuesday you wore a dowdy shirt and slacks, whereas the second time you could have been playing tennis at Wimbledon.'

'That's right. Any idea why?'

'Well, the first time Jeremy refused to let you go to the loo, whereas the next time you didn't need to go at all.'

'That's true. And . . .'

'I wondered if, the first time, you'd taken the chance of the great Dame's appearance to slip into her house and go to her toilet. You disappeared for a couple of minutes while she was prancing about finding the balls and lecturing Jeremy. I'm pretty

154

sure I was the only one to notice.'

'So . . .'

'So if you were in her house, you could have been the one that removed that government paper that caused all the fuss. But I've no idea why you'd do such a thing.'

'Think back a few years.'

I mused for a moment. Then it came to me. 'You've met Dame Carol before . . . you used to work in her office. Wait a minute, she accused you of leaking something to the media. And got you fired.'

I looked at her sharply. 'So all this was an act of revenge. You ruthless old thing.'

Fiona smiled. 'They'll eventually find the missing paper; it's hidden under her carpet. But I don't think her reputation will recover so quickly. "Wasting police time" is a serious charge that will hang over her for years.'

'But . . . you mean the whole thing was rigged?'

'Uncle Jeremy suggested it himself. He'd had a few run-ins with Dame Carol over the years. He knew I was fond of croquet. I don't think he realised how good I was. But he was glad of the excuse to break the greenhouse window as the trigger to bring out Dame Carol. It worked beautifully. And he never had much time for that gardener.'

There was a croquet lawn at my old school in York. None of us was very good but one year a friend and I were the school champions.

20. ANCIENT AND MODERN

It was the proud boast of Cambridge University Mountaineering Club – and hence its caving subsidiary - that no student would have to revisit an old challenge during their university career if they went on summer expeditions. This year – 1990 – the cavers had elected to go to the far north of Scotland and explore the Smoo Caves at Durness.

'But there's only a couple of caves there,' protested George Goode. She was a mathematician with no academic interest in caves, just a hunger, from time to time, to stretch herself in a tougher context. She had been doing some background reading.

'You mean, there's only a couple found so far,' replied Richard Thatcher, the Cavers' Chairman. He was finishing a PhD in geology: firsthand experience of the geology of Sutherland would add to its authenticity. 'But there've been suggestions there might be more. I'd like us to go and see.'

Most regular Club cavers had shared George's reservations and gone for caves elsewhere. In the end there were just four, three muscular men and George, who travelled the length of the country in Richard's old Allegro, squeezed in with masses of caving equipment. George was relieved that as the only girl she had a tent on her own. She would be able to slip away from the eve-

157

ning's drinking in the local pub – a traditional part of any caving expedition - and maintain a sensible sleep pattern.

It took two long days to reach the far northwest of Scotland. The distances weren't huge but the single-track roads, once they reached the Highlands, were slow. George was amazed at the grandeur of the mountains. During the journey Richard had expanded on his research and his dreams.

'The Smoo Caves are on a fault line in the geology and formed around a stream. They've been there since Neolithic times. Once the outer cave was half a mile long but the top nearest to the sea collapsed. What's left is still the biggest sea-cave in the UK, only now it's not so big.'

'Does the sea still reach it?'

'Only at very high tides. Mostly it's a freshwater cave. There's an inner cave with a waterfall, where the burn cascades in.'

'I believe there's another passage on the far side of that,' added George. She'd been doing her homework.

'That's why I brought the dinghy,' explained Richard. 'We'll get wet in the end but we don't want to swim before we have to. I'd like to know where that passage goes. If you look on the map there are thirty or forty metres behind, before the stream disappears from sight above, about which we know nothing. That's plenty of space for another cave – maybe one that was accessed by Neolithic man after the last Ice Age.'

That led on to discussion of what Neolithic man might have to store. The level of anticipation in the car rose perceptibly.

Two days later the mood barometer was falling. The first reconnaissance of the cave system had left them amazed at the size of the main cave – thirty metres high and fifty metres across - but disappointed that there was no waterfall in the cave beyond. They had reached the passage beyond that and traversed until it stopped, with a small flow of water coming out from under a massive slab of rock. There were, though, no obvious exits to explore. The party had walked along the coast for miles looking for alternative caving challenges; then withdrawn, baffled, to the Durness Arms.

Richard sought guidance from the barman as he bought the first round of drinks. 'So what's happened to the waterfall in the Smoo cave?'

'Pal, have you no' seen the weather here in the last six weeks?'

'Sorry, we only got here yesterday. What's the matter with it?'

'It's never rained once. The uplands are parched. And the burn that supplies the Smoo has practically dried up. There's no water in there to fall.'

Richard seized his tray of drinks and returned with this data to the party.

'It's a once-in-a-lifetime chance to try something new,' he enthused. 'If the burn's almost dry we might get into the caves from where it disappears above.'

But the others had been conversing with locals and had an alternative plan. 'There are other sea-caves on Cape Wrath. Surely we've a better chance of finding something new where no-one's been before?'

'But this idea can only be tried after weeks of dry weather. I bet that's almost unknown in these parts.' Richard turned to George. 'You've done some reading around this. Has it been tried before?'

George considered for a moment. 'Not that I can remember.

159

But we don't all need to try. You lads could go over to Cape Wrath while Richard and I'll see what we can do here.' She glanced down at her slender midriff. 'After all, if it's a matter of crawling down a tiny stream-bed then my size could turn out to be crucial.'

Richard was reluctant to split his party but everyone else seemed satisfied.

Next morning was fine and bright, scarcely a cloud in the sky. Richard took the other lads to catch a ferry to Cape Wrath. In the meantime George aggregated the most useful maps of the area. Together the pair scrambled over to where the burn – now a trickle – disappeared in the ground. Was the idea even possible?

'Hm. It's small enough,' said Richard. 'I'd just get stuck.'

He pondered and then turned to George. 'Trouble is, the burn might be low but it's still running. You might squeeze in – on the first part, anyway – but you're going to be soaked in icy water. Are you up for that? If you don't fancy it we could join the others.'

'I'll give it a go. Caving's not supposed to be easy.'

'You'll need to be cautious. If in doubt stay out. The Cambridge Cavers have not lost anyone since 1976 but if you get stuck I don't know how I'll get you out. Obviously you'll be on the end of a rope but that'll be no help once you're out of earshot.'

Eventually the pair concocted some emergency signals. Three sharp pulls on the rope, from either end, would indicate a need to return. Five would ask for a steady pull . With luck neither would be required.

Half an hour later, George had lowered herself into the burn opening and set out on her adventure. The aperture was rugged but by no means vertical. Despite a helmet with lamp, waterproof trousers and jacket, it was not long before the cold water had penetrated to her skin. Keeping moving, she decided, was the only way to keep the cold at bay.

She made sure she kept the rope slack. The thought that she might be the first person ever to come along this route was exhilarating but slightly frightening.

The shaft levelled out and for a short while she crawled on her knees through the water and under the low roof. Then the burn went into a small pool and disappeared beneath a massive slab. Could this be the other side of the slab she had seen the day before? It was hard to believe she'd come that far. But if she hadn't . . .all sorts of possibilities flashed through her mind.

Best to return to the surface and come back with breathing gear. But it all depended how far the slab scooped below the surface. If it was only a few feet she could swim beneath while holding her breath - worth a try anyway. Carefully she pulled the safety rope towards her: she needed some slack, she had no idea how far she would have to travel underwater.

For a few moments George mentally rehearsed her next move. She was confident that she could hold her breath – even in this cold water – for a minute and a half. She must turn back after half that time. She set the timer on her waterproof watch. She was starting to shiver: she needed either to go forward or return to the surface. She drew a deep breath and plunged into the pool.

What George had not anticipated was the cloud of mud stirred up by her entry. She could scarcely see her watch in front of her

161

face. On the plus side she was not restricted in her movements: the channel must widen beneath the slab. She swam steadily, hoping she was still on course.

Her alarm dinged. But she sensed the slab was rising away. She swam upwards and her head broke the surface.

She had reached another cave, possibly one never before seen by modern man.

There was just time, George decided, for a brief survey. Richard would be worried but cavers all knew that exploring took time. There were higher rocks to one side and with some effort – her muscles seemed weak - she managed to scramble up. There were no other ways in or out; her head torch was the only source of light. Slowly she shone it around.

This place had been used by ancient man alright. But not for storage, it had been used as a burial chamber. Everywhere she looked there were skeletons. It wasn't macabre; there was no deathly odour, just a sense of melancholy peace.

And then, at the back, on the highest ground of all, she saw remains that were far more modern. Amongst the bones was a leather belt . . . and off to one side a caving helmet that must have fallen off after death.

George had not been fazed by evidence of death from before the last Ice Age. But a recent death was much more disturbing. Now she wanted to get out of the cave system – and never come back.

Others, though, would have questions. This person's family would surely need peace and closure. Was there any clue on identity? She forced herself to go closer and look more carefully.

And to her horror saw a student scarf, with one end knotted amongst the bones and the other tied to a protrusion above.

But before she could do more, her rope twitched. Then came three distinct pulls. Richard was calling her back. She gave an answering pull. Then, with one final glance round the isolated cavern, she took a deep breath and plunged once more into the cold, dark pool.

She knew it would be hard work swimming back against the flow. But the current seemed really strong: it was much more of a struggle. George was just starting to panic when she realised that there was once more space above her. Relief: she could once more draw breath.

Now for the physical crawl through the tiny passage. There was much more water in the burn - this passage must normally be fully submerged. Now, if the flow was six inches higher, she'd be a goner. George wanted to pause but sensed time was precious. This was no time for reflection - or panic. She forced herself to battle steadily on, colder than ever, until the passage headed upwards.

Then, a minor miracle, she could see light above.

'Richard,' she screamed, 'can you help pull me up?'

'OK,' he shouted back, 'come when you're ready. I'll pull as hard as I can.'

Twenty minutes later, soaked, shocked and shivering, George was lying on the bracken beside the burn. The sun was no longer shining; heavy rain had taken its place. The long fine spell was over.

Richard observed her with concern. 'You need to be somewhere to dry out and warm up again.'

163

It was an extravagance but Richard had some funds for emergencies. Half an hour later George found herself in the Durness Arms enjoying a long, hot bath.

Over a belated lunch she told him of the burial cave. 'Richard, someone from recent times died there too. I was just starting to examine him when you called me back. I'm afraid . . . I'm afraid it was another student.'

Richard looked at her, distraught. 'I've spent the last hour on the phone, talking to my predecessor. The last death on a Cambridge caving expedition was when they came here in 1976. It was a small woman – "Shocker Shirl, the Newnham Girl". I gather she was an awesome caver, fearless, almost reckless. She went down the same way you did – she didn't know the rains were about to start either. But she wasn't so lucky.'

George looked at him in horror. Now she thought about it, it had been a Newnham College scarf dangling down. But would it help Shirl's family to know that in her final desperation, trapped by rising water, Shirl had hanged herself as an alternative to a lonely, lingering death?

George agonised over what to do: would Shirl's family want to know the whole truth or were they better left in blissful ignorance? They must already know she had died caving; did the final mechanics really matter?

In the end George never told anyone the details of her find. Once back from Durness, though, she resolved that she would never go caving again.

The entrance to Smoo Caves, Durness

21 NIGHT FLIGHT

T he small plane sounded as if it was in trouble. Its engine faltered and then roared again before once more losing power. Lower and lower it came, circling, looking for somewhere, anywhere, that was safe to land. But it was a bright moonlit August night and the Vale of Pickering was covered with huge fields of wheat or corn, almost ready to be harvested. No way to land there. One or two fields were grassy meadows but these were too small or else occupied by cows or other animals. What about the roads? The Romans would have despaired. The ones here were narrow and wiggled back and forth around medieval field boundaries.

The plane was losing height fast now, running out of options. Finally the pilot seemed to spot a field next to a farm which had been laid out ready for next day's horse trials. It was relatively flat and obstacles, if any, were tiny. The plane turned once more and headed in, lower and lower. At the last minute the engine faltered once again. It lost height suddenly and plunged into a giant haystack on the edge of the field. There was a muffled "boom" and then, a moment later, the whole wreckage was engulfed in towering flames.

Long before any fire engines were on the scene – and that took well over an hour - there was nothing but chunks of twisted metal and fragments of flame-engulfed material left to be seen.

My Inspector had collected me from the end of my night shift at

Scarborough Police Station. Jim Salting hailed from Essex and was as much an outsider as me, WPC Lauren Shaw, a girl with a Gran from Jamaica, whose Mum had later moved east from Bradford. Perhaps both Jim and I being outsiders to North Yorkshire was why I was his chosen bag-girl. Anyway, it was a relationship that suited us both. He had a huge amount of experience and I contributed occasional fresh perspectives.

'There's been a plane crash,' Jim told me, as we drove through the Scarborough suburbs in faltering first light, no-one else moving. 'On some farm near Helmsley.' He gave me an address and I plugged it into the Satnav. The machine deliberated: probably didn't like early Sunday mornings either.

'Almost to Helmsley,' I reported, 'then onto a small road past Wombleton. Why are we needed?'

'Fire Service called us. It took them an hour to get the blaze under some sort of control. There's been at least one death. I've no idea how we'll identify the body. Won't be much left to work with.'

He knew no more. And he had taught me "speculation without information" was a waste of mental energy.

We were at Albatross Farm an hour later. It was light now, men from two Fire Engines were still hosing the smouldering hay.

'We think he was trying to land in the paddock,' said the Senior Fire Officer. 'For some reason he came in too low and plunged into the haystack. No rain here for nearly three weeks: dry as a bone. The splattered air fuel was enough to cause an explosion and then it spread. 'Fraid there's not much left of the pilot.'

He indicated the dark mass of metal in the centre of the burnt area. 'It'll be a few hours, I'm afraid, before it's cool enough to get closer. And no, there's no clue on the identity of man or machine. DNA wouldn't survive that heat.'

Jim waved at the farm. 'Lucky it didn't hit the main building. I don't suppose anyone saw the plane on its way down?'

The fireman shrugged. 'Seems no-one here was at home. Maybe they were away for the weekend.'

'They'll have a shock when they get back,' I observed. It was hardly a riveting contribution.

Back in the car Jim found the number of Yorkshire Air Traffic Control and gave them a call. 'No, no plane had been reported missing,' they said. 'What time exactly?'

The Fire Officer hadn't been too sure. 'We were summoned from the phone box in Wombleton at 3:12,' he'd told us. 'But the caller sounded the worse for wear – probably staggering home after a long night out. I don't know how long before that he'd seen the flames; or how long before that the plane had landed.'

Jim talked into the phone. 'We're not sure yet. Early hours. We'll do our best to narrow it down,'

He made another call, this time to Scarborough, and put a request on the police media website: had anyone heard a light plane circling near Helmsley, late yesterday evening?

I hoped they had. Local enquiries round here could take me an age. I could only trust the media would do part of the job for me.

Later that day Jim and I were back at the site. There'd been limited response to our calls so far (to be honest, none). The Air Traffic Investigator was there now and looked rather baffled.

168

Jim made the introductions.

'It was a very intense fire,' we were told. 'Not just standard aviation fuel. It's really destroyed everything. All that's left of the pilot is a pile of charred bones.'

'Is there a Black Box?' I asked.

'They're not fitted on small planes like this,' the Investigator replied. 'In fact, it's hard to find any data at all. Not even sure of the plane's make. Not British, anyway. It might be Russian.'

'Was it not picked up on the UK Defence radar?' asked Jim.

'We've checked that. A small plane flying in very low over the coast might not be seen. There are one or two dead spots if you know where to find them. This one wasn't reported, anyway.'

It was sounding very mysterious – almost sinister.

Jim scratched his chin. 'But surely no one flies spying missions in the twenty first century? You could see all you needed from a dedicated satellite.'

'You'd still need a plane to bring people in,' I mused.

'Yes, but you'd also need somewhere to put them down. There've been no reports of odd landings at any airport in Yorkshire. I double checked with ATC.'

On Monday I was supposed to be off duty. 'I'll come in if you want,' I told Jim. I didn't want to miss out on any case developments.

'We're stuck for the moment, Lauren. I'm waiting on responses to my enquiries. Come back on Tuesday with a fresh mind.' Like I said, Jim was a good boss.

Actually, I did have an idea but it was a long shot. I had a cousin who lived in Kilburn – not the place in London, the small village just below Sutton Bank. A famous furniture maker once lived there – he scooped an intricate mouse out of each piece of furniture. Today his larger pieces – oak tables and chairs - sell for thousands. Nowadays his descendants ran the business; and my cousin, Henry, was on the payroll.

There was a regular bus from Scarborough to Thirsk that ran near Sutton Bank. I reached Kilburn late morning after the bus had dropped me. I had a walk along the edge of the scarp, with a view across as far as York Minster, then had to drop down past a huge White Horse that had been scooped out of the hillside turf.

As I walked I saw gliders taking off from a grassy airfield at the top of the Bank. They would start with a tow into the air from a small, single-engined Tiger Moth. The tow rope was released by the glider once they had reached a sufficient height. As long as they caught a thermal they could circle higher and higher into the sky. They didn't need to come down for ages.

One day, I thought, I'm going to have a go at that. It looked fun.

I'd warned my cousin I was coming to see him. He was pleased to see me. 'If you wouldn't mind waiting a few minutes, I'll take you for lunch in the Kilburn Arms,' he said.

It was a treat to sit in the corner of the workshop and watch a smooth running business operate.

The Kilburn Arms was a well-furnished inn. Now I thought about it the whole village looked remarkably prosperous.

'My treat today,' said Henry. 'It's been a while. Are you still playing cops and robbers?'

My career choice had prompted some disquiet among the

older members of my family but our generation knew that we had to make our own choices and then make them work.

'It's been fine so far,' I replied. 'I've got a good boss: we support one another.'

'So what's the latest riddle?' he asked.

He couldn't have set himself up better if he'd tried.

'Let's order and then I'll tell you. I need your help, if you don't mind.'

Twenty minutes later I was enjoying a cider while Henry supped a tomato juice – a bit of a surprise, then I remembered that he was still working this afternoon. Both of us had plates of posh salad.

Quickly I told him about the plane crash near Helmsley. It had been on the local television news anyway. I had no misgivings about betraying intelligence, in this case the police had none. It was all a great mystery.

'So how can I help?' he asked.

'It seems almost certain that the plane took off from somewhere local. There's lots of radar covering the County and it doesn't appear on any of it.'

'Yes?'

'Then I remembered the gliding club at the top of Sutton Bank. They were flying as I came past. Do you know if it operates at night?'

'I doubt it. Flying a glider is hard enough in the daytime. Not the flying, you see, it's the landing. You can't be sure you'll be on a proper, well-lit runway. It'd be no fun in the dark.'

'Well, if it doesn't run, is there anyone around that would notice a light aircraft landing and then taking off again there, if it happened in the middle of the night? I mean, how well is it guarded?'

'The Control Tower – such as it is - is kept locked. But they don't have any high fence round. I mean, why should they – it's only a field, there's nothing to steal. No-one leaves their glider there overnight. And there are no houses nearby.'

It sounded possible anyway. I would have something to tell Jim next morning.

Henry suggested I tried a different route back to the bus. 'There's a footpath that starts at the bottom of the hill near here. It runs through the trees, rising steadily – finally comes out on the main road, near the top of the Bank. Once you're near the top you should be able to see Lake Gormire.'

I decided to try it. There was no-one else on the path – perhaps because it was a Monday. The track was well-marked, anyway. I was almost to the top – I could see the gate to the main road not far ahead – when I came across the hut.

Or to be more precise, its remnants. It was a hut no longer, it had caught fire some time ago.

But not that long. There hadn't been time for any weeds to grow through the metal frame. Looking more carefully I saw it might once have been a small garage, maybe for a truck that worked in the surrounding forest. The two doors which would open on to the path had been badly singed but not completely destroyed.

I was in no hurry and stopped for a closer look. It was a bit of a struggle but eventually I manoeuvred myself round the side so I could see inside.

It looked . . . well, it looked as though someone had died in there. There was a bundle of blackened bones, lying on what might once have been a metal chair.

Quickly I pulled out my phone and called the police. Then settled myself on the path opposite, where I could await their arrival.

'I thought you were supposed to be off duty,' said Jim next morning as I went into his office. 'If you start finding bodies on your days off then you'll never make it to sergeant.'

But he spoke with a smile and was obviously pleased I'd been useful.

'I've just had a copy of the report from the Thirsk Fire Service,' he added. 'Plenty of people passed by on Saturday without reporting anything, so they reckon the fire happened on Saturday evening. The odd thing is, they say, there were traces of high octane fuel in the remains. That reminds me of the plane crash. No clue yet on identity of the body, but they reckon it wasn't the result of an accident.'

'Sir, the burnt-out garage wasn't the only thing I discovered yesterday,' I said, and went on to tell him about Sutton Bank gliding club.

Jim mused for a moment. 'If that was where the plane came from, is it just a coincidence it was so near a garage that was burnt out on the same evening? Is there any way the two are connected?'

I thought for a moment. 'There were the remains of a vehicle in the garage as well. Might that have been a getaway car?'

'If it was it failed pretty badly, Lauren. Didn't get away at all.

But could it have been a delivery vehicle? Bringing someone to the gliding club, say, ready for a night time exit?'

'Once they'd dropped him, they could have been told to stay hidden in the garage. But once the plane arrived, they could be done away with so they couldn't give anything away.'

It was a gruesome scenario but then we had two grisly crime scenes to make sense of.

'So your scenario, Lauren, is that the pilot bumped off the driver who'd brought him to Sutton Bank and then flew off. He might have been alright if the plane hadn't then crashed. On that basis the whole case has now been dealt with: one man murdered and the murderer then killed?'

'But sir, that doesn't make sense. There must have been some-one to fly the plane in to start with -'

I paused to try and work it through. 'Exactly how many bodies did they find in the plane when it came down?'

Jim searched his desk for a piece of paper. 'I ran off the report I got from the Air Investigators late yesterday. They say . . . they couldn't be certain but they could only recognise one set of bones left in the cabin.'

I was excited now. 'So the alternative is that there was a third person involved. He's the real villain. Someone who dealt with the driver who'd brought him to Sutton Bank and then later finished off the pilot. He might be still hiding near the plane crash.'

'If this person was fleeing the country, Lauren, they wouldn't hang around. It's over forty eight hours since the plane crashed.'

'But they didn't expect to be here, sir. They might not have the right clothing or maps – or even money. They probably hoped to be somewhere in Eastern Europe and now they'd lost the means to get there. And remember, they were in the crash as well. Who knows how badly injured that left them?'

'You might be right, Lauren. OK. Let's go back to the plane crash and have one more look round.'

I might be doing a house to house search of villages around Albatross Farm after all.

We started with the Farm. The farmer was back from his weekend with his relatives but had not seen anything. The plane wreck site was still circled with police crime scene tape, it looked rather forlorn. The Investigators had removed most of it, including the bones, on a massive truck.

Standing in the Paddock I suddenly remembered what the fireman had said about their call coming from Wombleton. This was the nearest we had to a witness. It would be good to meet them, I thought, to find out how close they'd been to the crash and what they'd actually seen. I suggested to Jim that we could start our enquiries in the village.

'If our theory is correct we're looking for a double murderer,' observed Jim. 'He's probably unarmed but you're not confronting him on your own.'

'We're only asking at doors, sir,' I replied. 'In the first place we're trying to find the 999 caller. If we stay opposite one another across the street we'll be safe.' Reluctantly he agreed and we set to work.

For a time it was all very tedious. No-one had seen anything. Then I came to a house with a "For Sale" sign outside. I was about to give it a miss, then I realised this might be exactly what our man (I'd dubbed him Moriarty) might go for.

Jim was still working the houses opposite. I gave him a wave and then strode up the garden path.

If Moriarty was inside I expected he would stay as still as possible until I'd gone away again. What I hadn't expected was that he would pull open the door as I walked up to it and drag me inside.

This was the point at which I should have shouted for help. But Moriarty gave me no chance as the front door was closed. He was immensely strong, tattoos down both arms, and had me down on the floor before I knew what was happening. My uniform, I realised, had given me away as I walked up the path.

When I'd joined the police I'd been taught self defence, but the lessons had not started with a bulky man already astride me. His desperation gave him strength. A handkerchief emerged from his pocket and was tied over my mouth. I was pushed roughly over on to my front. Next my wrists were hauled together and tied tightly behind my back with a piece of electric cable. The same thing happened to my ankles and then wrists and ankles were pulled tightly together. I was trussed up like a chicken.

What did he plan next? I saw him turn towards a rucksack standing beside the wall and pull out a large canister. He was going to set fire to the house! I did my best to wriggle out of my bonds but it was no use.

Then, out of the corner of my eye, I saw the front door inch silently open. It was Jim.

I had to distract Moriarty. With a supreme effort I pushed myself up against the wall opposite the door. Moriarty stopped for a second to see what I was doing. And as he did so Jim launched a flying tackle that brought him crashing to the ground. He tried to struggle but Jim was very fit - and very angry.

Ten minutes later Moriarty was seated on the floor, his wrists handcuffed behind him and legs tied to the staircase, as Jim called up reinforcements.

I never found out Moriarty's real name. Perhaps he was a spy rather than a master criminal. It turned out he had escaped from the High Security Jail near Wakefield on Saturday evening.

He'd had some help to get out. His friends had also organised a flight out of the country overnight, before the nation's Defence Forces were alerted.

Jim was commended for his efforts. I received a mild warning for putting myself in unnecessary danger. After all, Scarborough Police could hardly give both its "outsiders" a hero's welcome.

The Kilburn White Horse on the edge of the North York Moors

177

Made in the USA
Charleston, SC
24 September 2016